CU00657869

KNIGHT

City of Sisterly Love: Book 1

AK Landow

AK Landow

Copyright © 2022 AK Landow

All rights reserved

The characters and events portrayed in this book are fictitious. Any similarity to real persons, living or dead, is coincidental and not intended by the author.

No part of this book may be reproduced, or stored in a retrieval system, or transmitted in any form or by any means, electronic, mechanical, photocopying, recording, or otherwise, without express written permission of the publisher.

ISBN-13: 979-8-88680-476-8

I would like to thank my husband and children for supporting me in this new endeavor. I must also thank my good friends Stacey and Sherry for their loyalty, assistance and friendship. As my first beta readers, your feedback and confidence in me was everything. I appreciate you both. My final thanks goes to TL Swan. Without your Cygnets group, I would never hav mustered the courage to write this book. The plot has been bouncing around in my head for years, but your encouragement is what made m finally put pen to paper.

"A glowing woman can help other women glow and still be lit." ~Christy Cole

PROLOGUE

Darian

"Baby, I don't know how to be without you. How is it that you're no longer by my side? Why did this happen to us?" I sit with my elbows on my knees, looking at the fresh dirt that has just been thrown over my husband's coffin. Tears are free falling from my eyes.

Now that I'm finally alone with him, I remove my sunglasses. I'm sure I look a mess, but I really don't care. I'm only forty-five years old and my fifty-three-year-old husband dropped dead from a heart attack last week. I'm barely keeping my head above water.

"The service was standing room only. So many people love you and will miss you. I hope you know how much you are loved. You were, and will always be, my everything. I'm forever thankful for the time we had together. I wish it didn't end, but I will carry on for you. I will carry on your legacy through our children. I promise to come here every week and keep you up to date on everything going on with the girls and me. I can't believe how much you're going to miss in their lives." I pause as more emotion overwhelms me. He's going to miss so damn much.

"Harley, Reagan and Skylar all spoke so beautifully about you. They adore you. I will make sure they never forget you, and what an amazing husband you were to me, and father you were to them. We are all forever your girls." I take a breath.

"Alan and Nelson spoke as well. They told a few funny high school-era stories that had everyone laughing in between their tears. All of your friends have been amazing to me. They promised to take care of us."

I look back and I see my best friend Cassandra in a group   embrace with my girls as they head back towards me. I needed a few minutes alone with Scott today after all of the insanity of the past few days. Cassandra has been an amazing friend, holding us all together, and making the necessary decisions when I couldn't.

"Bye baby. I love you always. I'll see you next Friday." I blow him a kiss and turn as the girls return to me and hold me up, not sure I can even make it back to the car on my own. We hold each other up because we have to. Our rock is gone.

Now we will have to be each other's rocks. We collectively head to the limo to begin our new life without Scott.

CHAPTER 1

3 Years Later

Darian

"Hey, baby. I have some great news. We can officially call   Harley a doctor. She is now Dr. Harley Lawrence. She's passed her Boards and is starting her surgical residency this week."

I smile as a think of her in preschool, telling the teachers that she wanted to be a surgeon when she grew up. At a time when the girls all wanted to be ballerinas, she wanted to be a doctor. Not just any doctor. A surgeon.

"I'm so proud of her. I know you would be too. I'll give her the letter you left for her for the day she officially became a   doctor. She's excited to read it. Those letters mean so much to the girls." I pause and smile.

"You'd be proud of our babies, Scott. Reagan's new store is thriving only one year into things.

She has your savvy business mind. She's already talking about franchising. Skylar's final year of college has begun. She's still trying to decide whether to get her MBA or jump right into business just like Reagan did. She's leaning toward business school though. Just like her Dad. I'm so thankful that they're all close by." I couldn't have   survived the last three years without them. I live for them.

"Crazy Cassandra is trying to get me to go out more with her, Gennifer and Alexandra. We'll see. I know I need to get back out there, but I just don't know if I really want to. Do you think I need to get out of the house more? Do you have any thoughts on this?"

I look around searching for signs, but there's nothing except peaceful silence. I would love to hear either some thunder, or maybe a few extra birds chirping, to know he hears me.   Thunder for no, birds for yes. But I get nothing, per normal.

"Bye baby. I love you always. I'll see you next Friday." I blow him a kiss goodbye, and head to my car. As I get there, my phone rings with the tone of Aerosmith's "Crazy". Skylar programmed that in my cellphone for me as Cassandra's ring tone, and it's perfect.

"Hey, Cass."

"What's up, bitch?"

"Just leaving Scott and heading home."

"I assume to shower and get ready to meet us out at Cover Me," definitely said as a statement, not as a question.

"I don't know, babe. I'm not sure I'm up for it yet."

"Dare, you need to get out of your freaking house. It's ridiculous."

"I'm out of my house right now."

"You know exactly what I mean. Going to talk to Scott doesn't exactly count as getting out."

"I go out on Monday nights, September through December."

"Watching Monday Night Football with Scott's lame-ass group of divorced high-school friends also doesn't count. It's so weird that you do that. Why would you even want to watch so much football, let alone with a group of Neanderthals?"

She's never understood my inner tomboy. Growing up, I always preferred to hang out with the guys. She was probably my first true girlfriend. She also doesn't understand that spending time with Scott's closest friends makes me feel closer to him. She just doesn't get that part of me.

"After two years of mourning you promised you would start going out. I said nothing for two full years. I let you do what you needed to do to grieve and loved you through it. But a year ago, you said you were ready to get out and start living again. In the past year since, I can count on one hand how many times you've come out, and despite plenty of opportunities on those evenings, you wouldn't even talk to any guys. You can't be a hermit anymore. You've literally reached the end of Netflix. There's nothing left to watch. Don't even get me started on sex. Your vagina must be tighter than a virgin. You're a born again. Come on, Dare. It's time to move on. It's time to get out and meet people. You're still young. You're fucking gorgeous. Your enormous boobs still face the right direction. I love you. It's time. Do it before your boobs head south."

I feel the tears coming.

"Dare, are you there?"

"Yes, I'm here", I barely whisper.

"Don't fucking cry. It's enough with the waterworks. You've spilled enough tears for a lifetime. You need to get out and live your life. You need to have fun. You need to laugh."

"You need to meet someone. You need to fuck someone. And it's all happening tonight. Dare, you went from nympho to nun. Time to re-find your inner nympho. You were genuinely the only person I knew who had more sex in a week than I did, and now you've had absolutely nothing for three years. You must miss it. Come on. Come out with us. Put yourself out there. I will literally come to your house and drag you out if I have to."

I grip the steering wheel hard. The silent tears are now   streaming down my cheeks. "Cass, I just don't know if I can. I do miss that part of myself, I really do. But it would feel like it's   cheating on Scott. I can't explain it to you. I belong to Scott. I don't think I can be with another man. I can't fathom another man's hands on my body. That part of me may very well have died with him. It's been completely absent for three years. I don't know if I can find it. I don't know if I even want to." I take a breath.

"Cass, I haven't even touched myself since he died. My   sexuality is non-existent."

"You haven't touched yourself? What the fuck? You haven't had an orgasm in three years?"

"No. I think the old saying is true. If you don't use it, you lose it."

She scoffs at that. "Riding a dick is like riding a bike. Once you learn, you never forget how to do it. Come on. We're all on a mission to make you smile and get you laid. Time to rip off the band-aid, girlfriend."

"You're unbelievably relentless," I sigh. "Look, I'll come, but you can't just start pressuring me into meeting, and having sex with, random guys. That's not even how it worked for me when I wasn't broken. It's certainly not how it's going to work for me now."

"Fine, but if a good-looking guy comes on to you, you need to at least talk to him this time. And you're not broken. You just need a little kickstart. I'm an excellent kicker. I kick balls for a living." That's true, she does.

"Okay. I'll think about it." Maybe. Unlikely. "I'll see you at 7:00 tonight. Just remember that going out is a big deal for me. Don't make a whole thing about me meeting a man. I'm not ready to jump into the deep end. Baby steps, Cass."

"Sure," she lies. "Make sure that you grab an Uber. We're   definitely having several rounds tonight."

CHAPTER 2

Jackson

"Payton, where have you landed on the Abelson Proposal? Do you think we should invest?"

"Well, Dad, I think the properties look like a good investment. It's not such a great area, so we're getting in really cheap, but it's definitely up and coming. I think it will be the new Northern Liberties area of Philly. There are several new construction and development projects going on down there. In the next five years, I genuinely think it will be the place to be for twenty-one to forty-year-olds." I nod in agreement.

He continues, "location aside, I'm frankly just not sure that Abelson's guys know how to manage the project properly. After spending some time reviewing everything, and speaking with his team, I think we should counter that we'll help them fund the project, but we want to hand pick the management team and oversee construction ourselves. We need our people in there. I know we're stretched thin right now, but that's my assessment. I just don't trust his people to do this project right."

I look at my son and smile. "I came to the exact same   conclusion. If they want our thirty million dollars, they will do things our way, with our people, or they won't get a single cent."

I'm so proud of my son. He's smart and has a real mind for this business. Having him at only nineteen years old, he and I sort of grew up together. He's my pride and joy. I love that he now works for me. I take comfort in knowing that the business will one day be his and that it will be in great hands.

"Go call them and let them know what we're thinking. If they don't like it, too bad. They can find their funding   elsewhere. They'll give in. Trust me."

He nods. "Okay. I'll call them before I head out for the   evening. Do you need anything else before I go?"

"Oh, you're heading out?" I look at my watch. "I guess it's almost 7:00 already. I didn't realize the late hour." When you have no life and work is all you do, you don't pay attention to the time.

I look up at him. "Do you want to grab a drink

with me?"

"I would, Dad, but I really want to get home to Kylie. I only have her for another week or so before she goes on that ten-day cruise with her girlfriends." We both scrunch our noses. We hate cruises.

"We've never been separated that long since we started dating, and I'm going to miss her terribly." I smile at my son's happiness with his new bride.

"Newlyweds. I completely get it. Please go. Have fun. You can reach out to Abelson after the weekend, so you can get home to Kylie now. I didn't realize how late it was. Abelson can sweat it out for a few more days. Thinking we have minimal interest can only work in our favor during negotiations. I want you to negotiate this deal on your own. Do what you think is best for us."

Payton smiles. I've never given him this much autonomy. "Thanks, dad. Have a good night yourself."

He stands to leave, but before he exits, he turns back to me. "By the way, I think there's an Aerosmith cover band on at Cover Me tonight if you want to check it out. I know your old ass loves that old ass band."

"Blasphemy. Aerosmith is timeless. And I'm

forty-nine and can out bench press your youthful thirty-year-old body, so I don't want to hear the word 'old'. I'm hardly old."

I smugly smile at him and he laughs. "Thanks for the tip. Maybe I'll stop by."

Donna pops her head in as Payton leaves. "Will that be all for the evening, Mr. Knight?"

Poor Donna. I didn't even realize that she was still in the office. I'm about to let her know she can leave when the phone rings. Donna runs to my desk to grab it.

"Knight Investments, how may I direct your call?" She listens. "Oh, hello Mr. Clarrett." Donna has an evil genius look on her face. "Well, I think Mr. Knight may be in the restroom powdering his nose, but I'll check to see if he's available."

I look at Donna and smirk. She's a handful. I can hear him screaming at her to go and get me. She and I both silently laugh. What an asshole this guy is. I nod my head, indicating that I'll talk to him.

"Yes, Mr. Clarrett. He's done with his manicure so I suppose he can speak with you now." I laugh again.

I put it on speaker because I know that Donna will enjoy this. "Hey, Bryan. It's always lovely to hear from you. To what do I owe the pleasure?"

"You are a God damn motherfucker, Knight."

"Always the epitome of class, Clarrett."

"Cut your bullshit. There's a yet-to-be-named group buying up all of the properties around my Megaplex in North Philly. I know it's you and your cronies. What the fuck are playing at, Knight? I'm hearing all kinds of rumors. It better not be what I think it is. I've got everything tied up in this damn project. I don't need your meddling games. I will fucking end you."

"Hmm. I don't know anything about it, buddy. I'm happy to ask around though. You know, you should really better vet surrounding properties before you make that type of significant investment. If you worked hard and weren't handed your job by your daddy, as his second choice, of course, you would probably know that."

I love messing with this guy. He's such an easy target, and no one is more deserving.

"Fuck you, Knight. I know it's you. Don't push me. I'll push harder. You'll pull out of that project if you know what's good for you. You don't want me as an enemy. I play dirty."

Nope, I don't care. He knows he's not rattling

me, so he changes tactics.

"By the way, I saw your ex-wife the other night working the singles scene. She's looking mighty fine. No wonder she left your sorry ass. She was draped all over me. Couldn't get enough. She's probably never been with a real man." I can't help but laugh at that. She would never have interest in him.

"Melissa doesn't do bottom dwellers, Clarrett, but she's a free agent and can do what she wants. It doesn't bother me one bit."

Okay, it does bother me a little, but only because he's the biggest douche bag in town, and I don't want to see her mixed up with him. I definitely don't want her to be on his target list.

"Stay away from my shit, Knight. I'm telling you, don't push me. You won't like what happens." Without another word, he hangs up.

I turn to Donna with a smile. "Powder my nose? Manicure? Really?"

She shrugs and smirks at me. "It was the first mundane thing I could think of."

I adore Donna. She's become a close friend to me in the twenty-five years she's worked for me. I lost my own mother to breast cancer when I was a teenager, and at times, Donna acts as a bit of a de facto mother to me. I'm so thankful to have her in my life. Professionally, she's the best assistant around. I don't think I could run my company at this point without her. Personally, she calls me on my shit and sets me straight when I need it. She looks out for me too, sometimes a little too much.

As she's walking out, she throws in, "why don't you head to that bar Payton mentioned? Maybe you'll find a nice lady." She's always meddling in my love life. I know she   desperately wants me to find someone.

I roll my eyes. "I'm on a break from dating. It's more trouble than it's worth. The women I seem to meet are only   interested in my money and what I can do for them. There's no sincerity. I'm sick of all the lies and I'm really sick of all the games. Donna, I hate to break it to you but I may just not have been destined to have love in my life. Besides the boys, of course." My children are the most important people in the world to me. "I'm at peace with that. I need you to be too."

Donna looks at me like I'm a wounded puppy, with pity in her eyes. "You know, everyone gets a great love of their life. You're just going to find yours a little later than most. But I know it will happen, Jackson. You're a wonderful man. You're a loving man. You have so much love to give to the right woman. You just need to find her. She's out there. I know it will happen for you. I have faith."

Donna knows that while I loved my ex-wife Melissa in some ways, she certainly wasn't the love of my life. She fell   pregnant during our sophomore year in college so we married for Payton's sake, not for love. It was the right thing to do.

Once I eventually finished school and started my business, we were surprised with twin boys. And while I came to love and respect Melissa as the mother of my three amazing sons, I know I was never truly in love with her. We didn't have a great marriage. Not even in the beginning. In fairness, she wasn't truly in love with me either.

My marriage is my biggest regret in life. Not my sons, they are my everything. I'm eternally grateful for them. I regret not finding the right person to marry. It's a void that I don't know will ever be filled.

I'm forty-nine years old. I've sort of given up on the whole notion of having that one special person. I'm still a single man and have needs, but I've resigned myself to the fact that I will probably be alone for the rest of my life. I have my business and my sons. That will have to be enough for me.

I look at Donna so full of hope for me. She's been married to her husband for fifty years. I will never have that. I smile at her. "I don't know that the great love of my life will be hanging out at Cover Me tonight, Donna, but my second greatest love, whiskey, certainly will. For my second love, I will head to the bar." I wink at her. She rolls her eyes and walks out the door. Whiskey and Aerosmith, here I come.

CHAPTER 3

Darian

Cassandra, Gennifer and I have ordered our drinks as we wait for Alexandra. Cassandra is telling us about a tantric massage parlor in town that gives happy endings. She's apparently become a regular. We're all hysterically laughing at her antics, and we've only had two sips of our drinks.

Crazy Cassandra is just that, crazy. She's been my best friend since our freshman year of college and we haven't looked back. She always got me into all kinds of trouble. We'd dance all night at fraternity parties. We'd sneak boys into our dorm. We'd sneak into professors' offices late at night and steal exams. We've had to run from the cops on at least five occasions.

Despite some of the shared antics, we've had completely different paths with regard to men. I started dating Scott when I was only twenty years old, and he has been my one and only since the day we met.

In that same time, Cassandra has had three husbands, three divorces, and has probably slept with over fifty men. She's   unapologetically sexually promiscuous. She falls in and out of love depending on how the wind blows that day. But she's a happy, successful lawyer, and is the best friend a girl could hope for.

I love her like a sister, and she's supported me for the past three years like a sister would. She's stunningly beautiful, with short dark hair, piercing ice blue eyes, the body of a thirty-year-old, and is always dressed impeccably.

Gennifer is a law school friend of Cassandra's who has been in our inner circle for over twenty-five years now. She's got long red hair and big brown eyes. Her kids are teenagers, a bit younger than mine, having not had them quite as young as I did.

I didn't go to law school with them. I had Harley when I was only twenty-two-years-old. I slow played law school at night while being a mother, taking a few semesters off when I had both Reagan and Skylar.

Alexandra finally comes in and sits down looking exhausted. She's a younger attorney in Cassandra's office, and Cassandra brought her into our group about ten years ago. She's very tall with long blonde hair. She only got married a few years ago and had her daughter right away, but has been struggling to conceive this second time around.

We've had to watch her endure infertility struggles. My heart breaks for her. She's nearing forty and I know she's worried it won't happen for them. Gennifer goes to order our standard eight blow job shots when Alexandra tells us to order six. We all look at her with wide-eyed excitement.

"Ugh, don't look at me like that. It makes me feel pathetic. I could be pregnant, but I don't know yet if I am." She takes off her jacket and looks at us. "Do you want to hear a fucking crazy story? I guarantee that it's like nothing you've ever heard before." We all nod in excitement.

"So, I get up at 5:00 AM to go to work today. My bitch boss   Cassandra likes me in early." Cassandra smiles and winks at that.

"I wake Brent up to let him know we have an appointment at the fertility clinic at 12:30 today. I gave him *very* clear   instructions. At precisely 12:00 he needed to come home and jerk off into a plastic cup provided to us by the doctor. Once that was complete, he was to make sure to secure the lid tightly. I distinctly told him to then put the sealed cup into an equally sealed zip lock bag in case of spillage. I even handed him a fucking zip lock bag. He was to then put the bag with the cup in the front pocket of his pants, so it stayed as close to body temperature as possible. Then he was to meet me at the doctor's office for my Intrauterine Insemination procedure. They basically take the good shit from his sperm and inject it right next to my eggs to see if nature will then take its course. It eliminates the hard part, and the good part." She smiles at that.

"I've been on fucking Clomid all month, which stimulates egg production, and I have eight viable eggs this month. That means his sperm have eight possible destinations. If I'm the next octo-mom, I'm going to strangle someone, likely Brent. He claims to have come home precisely at noon from the office to jerk off. He gets into our bedroom and there's a cable guy in there. The cable guy says not to worry, that he'll be able to get HBO back and working, as if I care about HBO right now." She takes a breath, but quickly continues.

"Brent then seeks some privacy in our home gym, which he just then learns has a broken door lock. He's trying to watch porn on his phone, practically on mute so as to not alert   anyone in the house what he's doing, when he hears Rosie crawling up the stairs yelling 'dada dada' with my mother-in-law yelling at her, trailing after her. He realizes he can't   possibly get this done at home and he leaves. He remembers that in high school he used to jerk off in his car all the time, so he gives that a go. Except he's forty-two, not sixteen, and can't get it done. The guy can jerk off while my nipples are falling off breastfeeding Rosie next to him bed, but alone in the car, he can't get it done."

"He goes back to his office to use the private bathroom, which incidentally also has a broken lock, and allegedly finally gets the deed done. He shows up at the doctor's office forty-five minutes late. I'm fuming. I'm in a gown with my ass hanging out and I literally run into the waiting room yelling at him. I'm so mad that I don't even care anymore that everyone can see my bare ass hanging out. We get into the back room and he takes out the cup to hand it to the nurse. It's *fucking* empty. No sperm. Nothing. Side note, it's also not in a fucking zip lock bag because he can't fucking follow simple instructions. He swore the sperm was in the cup fifteen minutes ago. I've never been so angry and frustrated in my entire life, and I work for   Cassandra." I can see the anger is still fresh for her.

"I turn to the nurse and yell at her to give me a new cup and five minutes in a private room. On the way into the room, I'm yelling at him that this is clear a scheme to get a blow job from me in the doctor's office. We get to the room and he pulls his pants down. Do you know what I see?" We all shake our heads in shock at this ridiculous story.

"I see a big fucking wet spot on the side of his boxer shorts. Do you know why?" Again, we shake our heads.

"He didn't fucking secure the lid, per my instructions, and certainly didn't fucking use the zip lock bag, per my   instructions, so his sperm fucking spilled in his pocket and was all over his boxer shorts. I pointed at it and said 'I hope that was your son you moron'. So, I gave him a blow job, got it done in like two minutes, and then had the Intrauterine   Insemination procedure. I honestly hope I'm pregnant so I can tell this loving conception story to my child one day. Imagine 'conceived via blow job' on our birth announcements."

There's about a five-second shocked pause with all of us staring at her wide-eyed before we all snort our drinks out of our noses and are doubled over in laughter. I've never heard a more absurd story in my entire life. My sides literally hurt from laughing so hard. I honestly think this is the first stomach-hurting laugh I've had in three years and it feels good. Really good.

We ask a few follow-up questions to that crazy story as we wait for our shots, mostly about the logistics of medical office blow jobs.

We eventually have our two rounds of blow job shots, giving an extra cheers to Alexandra for already having done her fair share at the doctor's office today.

The Aerosmith cover band takes the stage and starts playing. Of course, "Crazy" is their first song. We all have to get up to dance to Cassandra's unofficial anthem.

We make our way to the dancefloor, and the four of us are   dancing and having a great time. This cover band is actually doing a pretty good job. A few unappealing men try to dance with us, but we shoo them away. Cassandra hasn't given me any grief over it, so I assume she agrees that they're unappealing.

After a few songs, the band slows things down with "I Don't Want To Miss A Thing" from Armageddon. Great song, but I'm not dancing to a slow song. This is my cue to leave the dance floor and grab another drink. I turn around to leave and bump right into a very broad and very solid chest. Without looking up, I mutter, "oh, I'm sorry. Excuse me."

I go to move around him, but he gently grabs my chin and lifts my eyes to his. They are a vibrant and penetrating emerald green, a shade I've never seen before. In a deep voice, he replies, "the pleasure is all mine. Would you like to dance?"

I'm caught a little off guard by the way this guy is looking at me. He's definitely attractive, but I'm actually out and having fun. There's no need for me to push things. I'm about to   decline, but before I can answer, Cassandra interrupts, "yes, she does."

CHAPTER 4

Jackson

I arrive at Cover Me a little after 7:00. The band hasn't even started. I take off my suit jacket and tie as I roll up my sleeves and order a double Monkey Shoulder Whiskey on the rocks.

My mind is on Bryan Clarrett. He's such a petty jerk. As young real estate investors both working for his father, he tried to undermine me in every single deal I was making. His father knew I had the better brain for the business and eventually offered for me to be his successor. I declined and went out on my own, but Bryan has never forgotten. This is the type of imbecile that coaches a little league team and benches my sons because of his beef with me. He hit on my wife constantly while we were married, just to get a rise out of me.

I smile as I think of the properties I now own around his Megaplex. Wait until he sees what I've got planned for them. He's going to really lose it.

After a few sips, I can finally feel myself start to relax. An attractive blonde, with big fake boobs, who doesn't even look old enough to legally drink, comes up to me. "Hey, handsome. Want some company? I'd love for you to buy me a Cosmo." Young is not my type. Fake is not my type. Asking me to buy her a drink is not my type.

I motion for the bartender to come over. As I'm ordering her a Cosmo, she goes to sit down next to me, brushing her body against mine as she does so. It does absolutely   nothing for me. I look at her and try to be honest. "I'm happy to buy you a drink, but I'm afraid I won't be very good   company tonight. I've had a bit of a day. Please take this drink on me and enjoy your evening." I smile at her. "You're very beautiful. I'm just not up for company tonight."

She grabs the drink while muttering "asshole" as she walks away. I shake my head and laugh. I can't win with women right now. I could have just been a dick and asked her to leave to begin with, but I was a gentleman and bought her the damn drink. That's all she really wanted anyway.   Somehow, I'm still the asshole.

Would she have rather I lied to her? I'm sick of this scene. I'm sick of the games. Are there any genuine and worthwhile women out there? I haven't met any. Perhaps I'm   looking in the wrong places. That woman was attractive and probably should have stirred something in me, but I felt nothing. What would she and I even talk about? Does she even know Aerosmith? It probably would have been an easy lay, but I feel like I already went through that phase of my divorce a few years ago. I'm just not into it. I'm giving up. I'm not ever finding the full package. I'm officially resigned to it.

I'm deep in my self-pity when I hear a table of women erupting into laughter and turn around to see the commotion. I scan the table and see that they're all actually very attractive, and shockingly seem age-appropriate for me. As I get to the last woman at the table, all the blood in my body rushes south. Holy shit. That must be the most exquisite woman I've ever seen. She's got chestnut brown hair with sun-kissed blonde highlights. It falls just past her shoulders. She's got green eyes, big lips and an hourglass figure that's got my heart beating fast. She either got the best boob job I've ever seen, or I've now witnessed perfection.

I need to adjust myself. I can't remember the last time I pulled semi from just seeing a woman. I'm about to go and talk to her when the band starts playing and her table jumps up to dance. They really seem to like the song

'Crazy'.

They're all laughing, clearly having a wonderful time together. I just watch her move for a few songs. Her gorgeous body moving to the music is so sensual. She's completely unaware of herself, making her all the more attractive to me.

I have to adjust my pants again before I embarrass myself. I feel like every man in here is watching her. Again, she's completely unaware of this. I've counted four men who have tried to dance with her that she has turned away.

I'm not sure I stand a chance, but I've got nothing to lose. I start to make my way over to her when one of Aerosmith's slower songs begins to play. This is my opportunity.

I'm entering the dance floor to ask her to dance, but as the song intro begins, she turns to leave the dancefloor and bumps right into me. She doesn't bother to look up as she apologizes for knocking into me.

I tilt her chin up so that her eyes can meet mine. As soon as they do her eyes pop wide open. They are so beautiful. A different shade of green than mine. I smile down at her and ask her to dance, but before she can answer, one of her friends answers yes for her.

I'm not looking a gift horse in the mouth. I signal my head towards the dancefloor and hold my hands near but not on her, silently asking for permission. She nods, so I put my hands on her hips and pull her close.

She is still staring up at me in the eyes, but eventually gains her composure and rests her hands on my shoulders. She's definitely keeping me as far away from her as possible, while still touching.

She smells amazing and I try to pull her in a bit closer, but she stiffens up. I bend my neck down to whisper in her ear. "Relax beautiful, we're just dancing here. My name is   Jackson, what's yours?"

She lets out a breath I think she was holding and smiles. "Sorry, I'm new at this." She must have just gotten divorced. "Nice to meet you, Jackson. My name is Darian." She relaxes a little and moves her hand up a little towards my neck. She feels good in my arms.

Darian

Jeez, this is the first time I've had a man's hands on my body in three years, and it actually feels really nice. And it's not just any guy. Jackson looks like he left a GQ model shoot to come here. He's one of the most attractive men I've ever seen in my life.

I'm a little happy that Cassandra interfered on my behalf and made me dance with him. He smells nice too. I haven't smelled a man's aftershave in so long. It's strangely comforting. He's tall, probably 6'2", and extremely muscular. He has thick jet black hair, shorter on the sides, and longer on the top. It makes those green eyes pop all the more.

He pulls me closer and I stiffen up, but I eventually relax and move my hands up from his shoulders to his neck. I close my eyes and let myself enjoy this much-needed fleeting moment of intimacy. I'll never see him again after this.

As the song ends, he doesn't pull away. He holds me close and bends his neck to whisper in my ear. "Can we sit and talk? I'd love to buy you a drink."

I pull away a bit to answer. "Thank you, but you don't need to do that. I'm actually here with some friends tonight, but I do appreciate the dance. It was really nice."

As if she was also dancing with us, Cassandra pipes up. "We don't mind. She'd love to have a drink with you." I don't even know where she came from. Was she standing next to us for the entire song?

He and I both smile at one another. "Well, apparently I'd love to have a drink with you,

Jackson."

He grabs my hand to lead me towards the bar, and again, the simple warm feeling of having a man's big hand holding mine does not escape me.

He motions for me to give the bartender my order. "Hey. I'd love a Tito's and club soda with several limes please."

Jackson smiles at me. "You need *several* limes?"

"A few simply aren't enough. Unless you say 'several', they only give you one or two, and that just doesn't get the job done."

Jackson's smile gets even bigger. It spreads throughout his entire face, right through to his sparkling eyes. What an attractive man.

He moves his hand and motions for the bartender to get him another drink. His exposed forearms are pretty damn attractive too. He asks the bartender to please send another round of drinks to my friends on him.

"That's extremely nice of you. Thank you. Bribing the girlfriends is a time-tested tactic."

He laughs and motions for me to sit, and I do. He does the same. "So Darian, tell me about yourself."

I probably shouldn't lead with the fact that I'm

a widow. It's kind of depressing. People assume when you're single at my age, that you're divorced. I'll stick with that for now.

"Well, I'm an attorney and I own a small law firm doing   corporate work. I'm only there part-time for the foreseeable future. I have a few associates who do most of the heavy lifting. I have three amazing daughters who are my everything." He smiles at that. "Harley is twenty-six and she's a first-year surgical resident. Reagan is twenty-three and owns a store down on Walnut Street. And Skylar is twenty-one and in her final year of college right here in Philly, likely applying to   business school for next year."

"Wow. That's incredible. All very accomplished. Congratulations to you. You must be very proud." I smile and nod.   "What store does Reagan own? Perhaps I know it." He seems genuinely interested.

"Tik Tok Trendy. She sells whatever the latest and greatest Tik Tok craze is. I don't get Tik Tok, but apparently, a lot of people pay attention to whatever they're peddling. It's actually been very lucrative for her." I'm rambling.

"That's wonderful. She's jumping in on a hot trend right now and taking it one step further. She sounds like a smart   businesswoman." He must be in business too. "Are you from this area originally?"

"No, I'm actually from the DC area. I came up here for college, and have been here ever since. Before you ask, I'm a huge Washington Capitals Fan. If you're a Flyers fan, we should probably part ways now. I can handle you being a Phillies and a 76ers fan, possibly tolerate an Eagles fan, but never a Flyers fan."

He laughs. "I'm actually from Colorado, so while I enjoy watching Philadelphia sports, the Denver teams have my heart. Be warned that I am an Avalanche fan."

"At least you're not a Flyers fan. The Avalanche are in the Western Conference, so we'd really only see each other in the Stanley Cup. I suppose I can live with that." We both laugh. "Tell me about yourself, Jackson."

"I have three kids as well, but all boys. Payton is thirty and works with me in real estate development. I own the company and my greatest joy in life is working with my son every day." I smile at that. I can certainly appreciate how wonderful that would be.

"That's very sweet. You have a thirty-year-old son? You don't look old enough to have a thirty-year-old son." That's the truth. He doesn't.

"I was actually going to say the same to you about your twenty-six-year-old daughter. You look way too young to have a twenty-six-year-old. My ex-wife and I actually fell pregnant our sophomore year in college, so we had him at only   nineteen years old. Seven years later we had our twins, Trever and Hayden. Hayden is just starting medical school and Trevor is getting his MBA in hopes to join Payton and me at our company."

"That's really nice. What a pleasure to be able to work with your boys. Though not as young as nineteen, I was pretty young when we had Harley. I was only twenty-two. She was a honeymoon baby. Maybe even a few weeks before the   honeymoon," I wink.

"Is your ex still in the area?"

Here it is. The dreaded question. The elephant dart to our   conversation. I take a breath. "I'm actually a widow. My   husband died three years ago."

His face drops. "Oh, I'm so sorry to hear that. It must have been very difficult for all of you."

"Thank you. Yes, it's been a bit of a long road, but here I am doing shots, dancing to Aerosmith on a Friday night, chatting with a handsome stranger." I'm trying to steer the conversation away from death as quickly as possible.

He smirks. "You think I'm handsome?" I give him a look as if it's not obvious.

He begins running his pinky along his lips as if deep in thought. For some reason, I find it extremely sexy. He has big thick lips. Women pay thousands of dollars for lips like his. And now I'm all of a sudden fixated on his lips. Oh jeez.

I've clearly not responded to his question, so he jumps back in. "I think you may be the most beautiful woman I've ever seen. Honestly, I couldn't take my eyes off of you all night." He gathers himself for a moment. "I'm sorry if that's a bit forward, but I can't help myself. You really are quite striking."

My lip trance is broken. "Thank you. I appreciate the   sentiment, but perhaps you need to get out more.

He leans forward into my airspace with a smoldering stare. "I think you need to look in a mirror more. You're stunning." Our eyes are locked with one another's. The mutual attraction is definitely there. I'm surprised at how I'm feeling right now. My heart is beating so fast in my chest. Words escape me.

He leans back breaking the stare down. He takes my hand in his. "Forgive me for being blunt, but I don't like to mix words. I like you, Darian. That doesn't happen to me very often. I'd like to take you out. Are you free next weekend?" I gulp. God, I haven't done this in a long time. He's certainly very good-looking, and I'm clearly attracted to him, but I don't think I'm ready to go on a real date. Talking to him tonight was actually a big step for me. Feeling something was even bigger. The physical expectations involved with dating may just be a bit too much for me at this moment.

"Jackson, I've genuinely enjoyed talking with you tonight. You're extremely charming and attractive. I imagine you have no trouble at all finding women that are interested in dating you. I just haven't gotten back on the dating horse quite yet though. I'm not sure I'd be good company. Frankly, I'm not one to have any interest in playing games or being disingenuous in any way. We're too old for that, don't you think?" He nods.

"I don't want to waste your time or lead you on. I'm telling you straight up that I don't know if I'm ready to date. You should find someone who is in a better head space. You deserve that."

"Wow, your candor is refreshing. I know you haven't been out there in a long time, but I promise you it's rare." He pauses for a moment as if thinking. Again, running that pinky along his lower lip.

"I'll tell you what. I will be away for work in New York all week. How about we simply talk on the phone? It's harmless. That should make you feel less pressured. If at the end of the week my amazing personality has won you over, you'll let me take you out next Saturday. If for some crazy reason you are immune to my charms, then we have each at least made a new friend. At a minimum, I'm always up for new friends. What do you think, Darian?" I blow out a breath. I guess this seems pretty harmless. No physical expectations on the phone. That and it will be easier to turn him down if I'm not looking at his gorgeous face.

"You make a very compelling argument. Are you sure you're not an attorney?" He smiles. "Talking on the phone? I think I can manage that. It sounds reasonable. Perhaps you won't like my personality by the end of the week and won't want to take me out anymore."

"I already like your personality, and I *know* that I want to take you out. I'm certain of that." Just like that, we're back to staring at one another in silence. "The ball will be entirely in your court though."

We end up talking a while longer, laughing and even flirting a little bit. Him flirting a lot more than me. We then exchange cell numbers, he kisses me on the cheek goodbye, says goodbye to the girls, and leaves the bar. The girls are all excited that I actually talked to a man. It's as if I'm fifteen years old and I just talked to my first boy. Cassandra is smiling from ear to ear.

They ask for all of the details. I let them know what went down. They continue yapping as we walk out together, but I'm not listening. My mind is on him. I'm equally scared and shocked that I'm actually attracted to him. I genuinely haven't been attracted to another man besides Scott in nearly thirty years.

When I get home that night, I get into bed with Jackson's smile and laugh on my mind. Maybe his eyes and lips too. It's stirred something in me that's been dormant for a long time. I don't know what to make of it.

My cell lights up with a text. I look over at my phone.

Jackson: Still thinking of you...

Yea, I'm still thinking about you too Jackson. I don't reply, but I can't get him out of my mind. For the first time in three years, I slip my hand into my underpants and touch myself.

CHAPTER 5

Jackson

Sunday Night

I get into bed at my hotel and dial Darian's cell number. I've been thinking about talking to her all day. She answers right away. "Hey there Aerosmith fan. How's the Big Apple treating you?" I laugh.

"Hey, sugar. Sorry I wasn't able to call yesterday. I didn't get to the hotel until late and didn't want to wake you. I've been crazy with meetings all day today, but I've been very distracted thinking about a certain gorgeous green-eyed brunette."

She doesn't respond so I try to lighten the mood. "To be honest, there's one question I have that I can't seem to move past."

"Oh really? What's that?"

"Why are you an emphatic Washington Capitals fan, but not as much so for the other

DC area teams."

She laughs. "I hope you didn't hurt yourself overthinking this. I mean I like the other DC area teams, but the Caps just have a special place in my heart. My father used to get a partial season ticket plan, which came to about twenty games. He had two tickets per game. As soon as we knew which games he was assigned each season, my brother and I would have a draft as to which games we'd each get to   attend with my dad. It was our special time with him. Even when we got older and he said we could take our friends instead of him, I always chose him. Seeing the Caps play automatically makes me think of my father and our special times together." That's a pleasantly endearing answer.

"That's really nice. What great memories you must have of those games. Is he still with us?"

"He is. I watch almost every game and he and I text   throughout each game. It's kind of our thing. I also got to spend the past twenty years bearing witness to the greatest hockey player of all time."

"I hate to break it to you, but Wayne Gretzky retired in 1999." I have a feeling this will rile her up.

"You can't think that Gretzky is better than

Alex Ovechkin. Ovi is the best of all time. Do you even understand hockey?"

I laugh. She knows her hockey. "Gretzky is still the number one goal scorer of all time." I'm thoroughly enjoying getting her riled up.

"Ovi is like two seasons away from breaking that record, but do you comprehend how much harder it's been for Ovi to get there? Goalies were half the size when Gretzky played, and the equipment was half the size as well. Ovi will have the record number of goals while having the goal covered double the amount of what Gretzky encountered. It's kind of a no-brainer."

"Gretzky won four Stanley Cups. Ovi only has one."

"Ugh. You bother me. We're over," she teases.

I laugh. "So you admit we're together? Perfect."

"No no no. I admit no such thing. If you decide that Ovi is the GOAT, you may call me tomorrow night. If you're stuck on Gretzky, I'm blocking your number."

This girl makes me laugh. She's adorable.

"Okay, Ovi is the GOAT."

"That's much better. Actually, if you do call tomorrow, please call a little later in the evening."

"Do you have big plans? A date?" I hope not.

She chuckles at that. "No no, nothing like that. I watch Monday night football with Scott's old high school friends. Scott was my husband. It's kind of become our tradition since he passed. I think it's their way of keeping an eye on me."

"That's sweet of them. What a nice tradition. It should be a good game. Have fun."

"Sweet? No. They're trying to pick my brain because I kick their asses every year in our fantasy football league."

"Oh, I need help with my team. I'll pick your brain on Saturday night."

"I haven't agreed to go out with you on Saturday night."

"We'll see."

Monday Night

I dial her number and she picks up. "Hey there." She sounds sleepy.

"Hey, sugar. I hope I didn't wake you. How was football with the boys?

"No, I'm up. It was fine. I was a little distracted tonight. I was actually mentally running through my past visits to Colorado. I used to ski there as a kid with my family nearly every year.

It's so completely different than Philadelphia. You must miss it."

"I do miss it. Nothing beats the Colorado skies. I visit when I can. Usually around the holidays. Maybe a few times a year depending on the year. My father still lives there, as does my oldest friend and his family. My boys all know how to ski. They won't even consider skiing on the east coast."

"What about your mother? Does she still live there too?"

"She passed when I was a teen. Breast cancer. She fought hard, but lost the battle in the end."

"I'm sorry to hear it. That must have been hard." It was. "Did your father remarry?"

"No, he's dated a few women, but never remarried. They were very much in love and he's never found that with   anyone else again. He lives alone. I worry about him."

"You sound like a thoughtful son. I'm sure he appreciates it. What do you miss most about Colorado?"

"I miss the mountains, the peace, the active lifestyle, the skiing, the hiking, the rafting. I miss seeing stars through clear skies. If I had to pick one, I'd say the skiing. Nothing beats the Colorado slopes."

"I haven't skied in years."

"Why not?"

"Scott wasn't a skier. We went on a few vacations when the kids were younger because I wanted them to learn, but then we kind of abandoned it for warmer weather vacations. I won't lie. I do love Mexico. Give me a few drinks, a beach chair and my Kindle, and I'm a very happy woman."

"Everyone loves Mexico. What's not to love? I'll take you   skiing sometime. Maybe to Mexico too."

"I haven't even agreed to a date. I think you're getting *way* ahead of yourself."

"We'll see."

Tuesday NIght

"Hey there Jackson." I can almost see her smiling through the phone by the tone of her voice.

"Hey, sugar. Can we FaceTime? I kind of want to see your face tonight."

"I'm not dressed."

"That's quite a visual. Now I'm hard." Thankfully she laughs. "I feel your state of dress right now is potentially a reason we *should* FaceTime."

"Not today."

I won't push. "Okay. Hmm. What to talk about tonight? Why don't you tell me your one party-ready fun fact conversation starter."

"Well, people seem to get a kick out of the fact that I was a Division One softball player."

"Really? That's amazing."

"Yep. First Team All-Conference."

"Impressive. You'll have to join our company team. You can be our ringer. No one will see you coming."

"You, Jackson Knight, are not the first person to ask me for that. I've been used as a ringer for years. What's your party-ready fun fact?"

"Let me think. I'm not that interesting."

"I doubt that."

"I know. I can juggle."

She laughs. "No, that's boring. Give me something better. More exciting. Something that sets you apart from all of the others."

"Well, I have a very large penis."

She's now hysterically laughing. "Oh my God, I can't believe you said that. It can't be as big as your ego."

"It is."

Wednesday Night

"Hey there."

"Hey, sugar. How was your day?"

"I worked today. It's good to get into the office now and then. I like to make sure things are running smoothly. I haven't been in much of late, so it was nice to see everyone. I haven't seen my girls all week though. I miss them. I won't see them until Sunday."

"Do you see them a lot?"

"I do. Usually at least twice a week. Sometimes they tag team checking in on me. I pretend not to know why they randomly drop by, but I do. And I appreciate it. We try to have Sunday dinners all together every week too. It's our collective catch-up time. What about your boys? Do you see them a lot, besides Payton obviously?"

"Maybe every other week right now. They're busy with grad school. And they have to split their family time with me and their mother. Though sometimes we all go out together."

"I assume their mother is local?"

"She is. She lives in the city now. She has a condo. She prefers the city life."

"If you don't mind my asking, why did you guys get   divorced?"

"I guess we're getting a little deep tonight. If I'm truly being honest with myself after years of reflection, we were never really in love. We got pregnant at nineteen and both did the right thing for Payton and got married. I don't regret marrying her, but I regret marrying out of obligation, not love." That's the truth.

"She worked her ass off and supported us while I   finished school, started working, and eventually started my   company. I will always have some amount of love her for that and for giving me my three boys. We just never had the all-encompassing, can't live without each other love. If you don't have that foundation, the small things add up and you end up growing apart." It's sad to say that out loud.

"We've been divorced for over five years, but we were mostly just cohabitating for years before that. We kind of had an unspoken understanding that we'd stick it out until the twins graduated high school. By then, even the boys asked us to get divorced. We're both happier now. It was completely amicable. We didn't even bother with our own lawyers. We just split everything right down the middle and each went our separate ways. We both love our boys and we'll always have that common ground. The boys were eighteen by then, so we had no custody issues."

"At least you had an easy divorce. I've heard some horror stories. I'm sad for you that you didn't get to marry for love. Everyone should have that. It must have been lonely." It definitely was.

We're silent for a moment. I know she's anticipating that I'll ask about her marriage, but I can tell she doesn't really want to talk about it with me, so I don't. "Sugar, I'm really beat. Can I call you tomorrow night?"

"Of course. Have a good night, Jackson."

"You too."

Thursday Night

"Hey there."

"Hey, sugar. I hope you had a good day. Tonight, I want you to tell me about your best friend."

"Well, you met Crazy Cassandra. She's my forever best friend."

"She's the one who *made* you dance with me, and *made* you have a drink with me?"

She laughs. "That's the one. She was my roommate our freshman year of college and we've basically been inseparable ever since. She's the most wonderful, amazing, loving, crazy friend you can ever imagine. I adore her. My girls think of her as their aunt, even calling her Aunt Cass. She's truly family to us, especially the past few years."

"Tell me one reason she's wonderful and one reason she's crazy."

"She's wonderful because she's held me up for the past three years when I could barely stand on my own. When I couldn't get out of bed, she made me. When I ran out of tissues, she got me more. When I couldn't mother, she mothered for me. When I couldn't sleep alone, she slept with me. After Scott died, I had trouble sleeping in the empty bed. She slept in my bed with me every night for a year because she knew what I needed. I will never be able to repay her for what she's done for me. As for crazy...hmmm... there's so damn much. I'm not sure I can pick just one."

"Try. I need to see if her nickname is earned"

"It is. I promise." She's silent for a beat. "Oh, I've got it, but you can't tell her that I told you."

"I won't."

"Promise?"

"I promise. I will even pinkie promise." I smile at that.

"She loves to tape herself having sex. She has a collection of thousands of videos of herself having sex with all kinds of men." She's giggling. "I can't believe I told you that. She'd kill me."

"She better hope that collection is never found."

"I honestly don't think she would even care. She's kind of unapologetically herself. It's actually very endearing. I love that about her." She pauses for a moment. "Tell me about your best friend."

"Payton is my best friend."

"That's sweet. It really is nice that you're so close to your son and work together every day."

"It is. I had him so young. In a way, we grew up together. He just got married. His wife's name is Kylie. They're an amazing fit and very much in love. I'm so happy he found that." When I didn't. "I feel they are one minute away from making me the youngest grandfather of all time."

"At least you'll be the hottest grandfather in existence."

"This is good. You think I'm hot. Is GILF a thing?"

She laughs. "I have no doubt that you'll make it a thing."

"Well, I suppose you're the authority, being a MILF and all. Perhaps we can make a club."

"Sounds like a plan. Any other friends? I know you   mentioned the other night that you still keep in touch with a friend from Colorado."

"I guess my forever friend is William. We've been friends since preschool. We've been on different paths, but have   always managed to stay close. He and his family live just outside of Denver, but I see them whenever I visit. I love his family. He has not had much career success, but he's been successful in love. In that regard, I'd switch places with him in a minute."

"You, Jackson Knight, are a bit of a romantic, aren't you?"

"Maybe. Just calling it like I see it. He has such a wonderful marriage. I'm both happy for him and envious of him." I need to change topics. I'm hesitant to ask the next question, but why not. "Can I ask you a risqué question without you getting upset with me?"

"You can ask it. It doesn't mean I'll answer it."

"Fair enough. Are your boobs real?"

She bursts out laughing. "So much for being a romantic. Why do you ask?"

"Because I can't stop thinking about them. They're perfect."

She's silent for a moment. I hope that wasn't too much. "Well, I guess I should say thank you then. They're real and they're spectacular." I can almost see her smiling through the phone.

"Seinfeld fan, I see?"

"I can speak in TV and movie quotes all day long."

"I can't wait to see how spectacular."

"We'll see. I don't know that you've won me over just yet." I have.

CHAPTER 6

Darian

Friday

"Hey, baby. It's been kind of an interesting week since I last saw you. I haven't seen the girls at all. They're crazy busy, but we're having dinner together on Sunday. We're meeting down at school so Skylar doesn't have to take the train. I still need to give Harley your 'When You Become A Doctor' letter. She's really excited to read it."

I kick a few stones nearby, nervous for what I'm about to tell Scott. "I kind of met someone, and I'm thinking about having dinner with him tomorrow. He's really nice. Everyone seems to think I should go out with him. Even the girls gave me the green light. Do you have any thoughts?"

I look around for a sign. Nothing. "One day you'll let me know your thoughts when I ask," I mumble to myself. "I miss you. I've been so lonely. Maybe I need to think about not being so lonely anymore." I look up and take a breath. "Bye baby. I love you always. I'll see you next Friday."

Tonight will be our last call before our proposed date. Our   conversations have been fun. They've gotten a bit flirtier and dirtier. I've enjoyed talking to him. He's a nice guy.

I haven't completely decided whether I should go out with him, but I'm leaning towards yes. I feel like I need to see this through to continue my healing process. I've been stuck for a long time. I'm nervous though. I'm scared too. This has been so much easier on the phone. No physical expectations. That's what's got me the most nervous. I'm definitely attracted to him, and I like his personality, but I don't know that I'm ready to get physical with another man yet.

Friday Night

"Hey there"

"Hey, sugar." I love when he says that. It makes me smile. No one has ever called me sugar. "Are you excited for tomorrow night?"

"What's tomorrow night," I tease.

"You know what tomorrow night is."

"I have not yet agreed to go out with you tomorrow night. I'm still deciding if I like you."

"You like me, I can tell. We're going out. It's

been decided." Cocky bastard. "I'll let you in on a secret. It was decided the second I laid my eyes on you last Friday night. You were always going to go out with me." He's in a mood tonight.

I let that go for a moment. "So… Cassandra kept telling me to Google you but I didn't want it to cloud my judgment this week, so I didn't do it…"

"Good."

"…until today."

"Oh boy. Here we go. Don't believe everything you read."

"You're kind of a big deal, Jackson."

"I've made a few smart investments. It's meaningless." It's more than a few smart investments. He owns half of   Philadelphia.

"It's not just your obvious career success, which is amazing. You're listed as one of the top ten bachelors over forty in   Philadelphia." I nearly fell out of my chair when I read that.

"It's hardly an accomplishment. My assistant made me do that photo shoot. I think there are only like eleven single guys over forty in Philadelphia, and the eleventh is a bit of a troll if you ask me." I laugh. I do like that at times he's confident, yet at other times there's at least some humility and self-deprecation in there.

"Ha ha, very funny. I don't think I can compete with your fan club. It must be quite large."

"There's no fan club and no competition. If there was one, you would have already won it." He can be so sweet sometimes. He's good for my ego.

"I have to tell you, in all honesty, I've jerked off more this week thinking of you than I have in the past ten years combined." I almost spit out my drink. So much for sweet. That's quite a statement. Though I'm all of a sudden finding myself a bit flushed. Even turned on. So much so, that I can't manage to reply to that. I don't know why the thought of a man that looks like Jackson touching himself to me is turning me on, but it is.

No doubt he can hear my breathing get heavier. He breaks the silence. "Darian?

"Yes, Jackson."

"Have you touched yourself this week thinking of me?"

Hesitating for a moment, and deciding to be honest, I whisper, "I have."

"How much?"

"Every day." I hear his breathing pick up. I close my eyes.   "Multiple times, every day." I hear him gasp.

We're both still breathing somewhat loudly, but otherwise on the phone in silence when I hear my doorbell ring. It breaks me out of my trance. I quickly ramble out, "someone is at my door. Text me a time for tomorrow night."

He doesn't say anything, so I just hang up. That got awkward quickly.

The doorbell rings again, reminding me to go answer it. I open the door and he's standing there. Oh dear God, I don't think I adequately remembered just how gorgeous he is.

He's standing there looking like he's about to combust. He walks in still staring at me, without saying a word. I move backward until I feel my back hit a wall. He moves closer, grabs my cheeks, and presses his body against mine. This feels too good. I was already worked up from our phone call, and this is escalating it even more.

We're both breathing heavily, looking straight into one another's eyes. He opens his mouth, mere inches from mine. "If you don't want me to kiss you, speak now." I can't get any words out. I don't want to let the words out. When I don't reply, he closes the final gap and crashes his lips into mine. His big, soft, juicy lips taking mine with such authority. His tongue begs entrance into my mouth and I open. It's such a perfect mixture of lips, tongue and suction.

I moan into his mouth which seems to excite him more   because he grabs my legs and wraps them around his body. I can feel how hard he is against me. Oh God, this feels so good. It's been so long since I've felt a man between my legs. I feel like I've been walking in the desert and just found a bottle of water. I may need more than one bottle though.

My body is an inferno. He can probably feel my heat and my wetness through my jeans. We keep kissing and kissing and kissing, until we are completely panting and out of breath. He drops my legs to the ground and I slowly slide down his body, feeling every hard inch of him.

He holds his forehead to mine with our breathing intertwined. "I'll pick you up at 7:00 tomorrow night." With that, he turns, walks out the door, and closes it behind him.

My body slides down the wall until my bottom hits the floor. I put my hand to my swollen lips. What. The. Fuck. Was. That.

CHAPTER 7

Darian

When I wake up the next morning, Cassandra is asleep in bed next to me. I left her a hysterical voicemail last night after Jackson left. She texted a short while later that she was on a date, and would call me when it was over. I fell asleep and probably missed her call.

She's still in her clothes from last night, at least her top. Her pants must be on the floor somewhere. Of course, she came. She's always here for me. She rolls over and opens her arms for me to snuggle in. I lay my head on her and let her embrace me. The waterworks start as I grab onto her. "What happened, Dare?"

"He kissed me."

"Who kissed you?"

"Jackson, of course."

"I thought he was out of town."

"I guess he came back. He just showed up. He

walked in   without saying anything, pinned me against the wall, and kissed the shit out of me. When we were done, he said he'd pick me up at 7:00 tonight and left without another word."

"Shit. That's fucking hot. How was the kiss?"

A sigh. "Good. Like really good."

"So why are you crying?"

"You know why. I don't know that I'm ready for this. I was out of my mind when he walked in. I think I would have let him do anything to me at that moment." And I mean that.

"And?"

"And I'm not ready. I can't cheat on Scott. I think I need to hit the brakes. Maybe we should just slow things down and   continue to talk on the phone. Judging by last night, I don't know that I can be trusted when I'm around him. He gets me all worked up."

"God damn it! You're not cheating Scott. I love you, but Scott is dead. He's been dead for three years. Your vows were 'til death do us part'. Your conscience is clear. You're forty-eight years old. You're not a high school kid with rules about how far you should go and when. If you want Jackson, take him. Fuck his brains out. Your body must be starving for it at this point." I think it is starving for it.

"Up until three years ago, you were the most sexual person I had ever met. And that's saying a lot coming from me. You could barely go twenty-four hours without it. I miss that   Darian. I miss talking to her. I miss hearing her laugh. I miss hearing about her sexual escapades. I promise you that Scott would not have wanted you to become an agoraphobic nun. He'd want you to be happy and living life. If it's permission you need, I'm here giving it to you. If it feels good, do it."

I'm such a mixed mess of emotions right now. In my head, I know she's right. I look down for a moment and then back up. "Maybe. I'm trying to wrap my mind around the possibility. The fact that I'm even considering it is progress, isn't it? Baby steps, Cass."

I lay back on my pillow and take a deep breath. We lay in   silence for a moment. Eventually, I turn back to her. "Sorry I cock blocked you last night. How was the date otherwise?"

"You didn't cock block me. We just had sex in the alley outside the restaurant after I told him that I didn't have time to come back to his place. It was actually pretty good. I'm always up for some hot alley sex. I have it on video if you want to watch it." We both start laughing hysterically at that.

"Your whole video thing is weird. I don't get it.

How often do you even watch them?"

"All the time. It helps me work on my technique." She managed to say that with a serious face. We laugh again.

"You must be an expert by now then. I don't need to see it. I would be okay watching people fuck in an alley, but I think I'm set on watching *you* do it. I've caught the live show one too many times." I've caught the live show a hundred too many times.

"Whatever. Our bodies are made for pleasure, Dare. I like to feed the beast. You used to as well. Time to wake up out of your self-imposed coma."

She's right. I need to move forward. I sit up and turn to her. "Help me pick out something sexy to wear tonight."

"That's my girl."

It's 6:45 and I'm ready for my date. Cassandra made me go out and get everything waxed, bleached, nipped, tucked, and everything in between "just in case." Jackson texted during the day to let me know I could be casual. I was perfectly fine with jeans and a sweater, even a tight sweater, but Cassandra was a hard no on that. She said that sexy and flirty were a must for a first date with a man that I know I'm attracted to.

I'm in a plaid pleated skirt. It's a bit short for a woman my age, but I do have long skinny legs, so here I am in a school-girl-looking skirt, with knee-high boots, and a very tight v-neck sweater that more than shows off my ample breasts. If I wanted to convey "slow it down," this isn't the outfit for that.

I'm downing my second glass of liquid courage when I decide to go get changed. I can't wear this ridiculous outfit tonight. How do I let Cassandra talk me into this shit? Unfortunately, before I reach my bedroom to change outfits, the doorbell rings. Shit, it's too late to change. Here we go.

I go to the door and open it. Jackson is standing there with flowers, wearing dark jeans, a black v-neck shirt, and a blazer. He literally looks like he just walked off of a modeling runway. He's so damn handsome. He scans my body and smiles. When his eyes re-find mine, I breathe, "hey, Jackson."

"Hey, sugar." He smiles warmly, wraps one arm around me and bends down to kiss me on the lips. It's closed mouth and soft. "You look stunning. I'm not sure we'll even make it out of here for dinner."

I glance at him. "We will *definitely* be making it out of here for dinner. Don't worry about that." Yep, I could totally see not making it out of here.

The chemistry I remember from last Friday is still here. I blink my eyes and redirect, "are these flowers for me?"

"They are." He hands them to me. They're tulips, which are my favorite. That's not a normal date flower. Clearly, he's done his homework. I may have to inquire about that, Cassandra.

"They're beautiful. Thank you. Let me put them in a vase and we can go." I walk into the kitchen to grab a vase and fill it with water. He follows me inside and into my kitchen. He looks around.

"Your place is really nice. The open modern layout is great. I'm seeing it in all of the new properties right now."

"Thank you. I moved here about a year or so ago. I needed a change of scenery." He nods in understanding. The truth is that being in the house that I shared with Scott became unbearable. Too many memories and too many 'what ifs' for me in that house. Finding him collapsed in our family room didn't help matters either. I couldn't even go into that room for months. Everyone seemed to agree that I needed a fresh start somewhere new that he had never lived. It took me a while to agree, but I finally did.

After I finish with the flowers, he takes my hand, "ready to go?"

I smile at him. "Yep, let's do it."

The conversation in the car is easy. He fills me in on his trip to New York. He's developing some properties up there. He tells me how Trevor has always wanted to live in New York City, so he's trying to build a portfolio up there for Trevor to eventually manage after he finishes his degree and learns the business. He's obviously a thoughtful father.

We walk hand in hand into the restaurant. I'm surprised to see that it's actually a bit of a hole in the wall, but when we walk all the way in, I'm taken aback. It's so charming. It's dark with a small stage. It looks like an old-school comedy club. "What is this place? I've never been here."

"It's a jazz club. I love it here. I can sit and listen to them play all night. The music starts playing in about an hour. I figured we can chat while we have a few drinks, and eat some food before they start. Then we can just relax with drinks and listen to the music." That actually sounds really nice.

The maître d' greets us warmly. He clearly knows Jackson and is happy to see him. "Your usual table is ready for you, Mr. Knight. Sabrina will show you to your table."

Jackson puts his hand into the small of my back to lead me to the table. He has touched me every second since we left the house. He held my hand to the car, in the car, into the   restaurant, and now his hand is on my back.

The hostess leads us to a semi-circular booth where we sit next to one another. Jackson immediately puts his arm around me and pulls me close to him. I shut my eyes at the closeness. I take in a deep breath and then exhale. That may have been a mistake. He smells amazing and it's overwhelming me.

I turn to him. "Your 'usual table'? Is this where you bring all the ladies from your fan club," I ask cheekily.

The corner of his mouth rises. "I've actually never brought a woman here. I usually come here by myself just to relax. It's kind of my happy place to get away from the craziness of life. Sort of like Caps hockey games with your father is for you."

I'm a little surprised at everything he just said. He's never brought a woman to his happy place until me, and he   remembered what I said about the Caps games with my father being so special. He definitely listens to me when I speak.

The waiter comes to take our drink orders. Jackson orders himself a whiskey and me a Tito's with club soda and *several* limes. He looks at me when he says the word "several". We both smile.

When the waiter leaves, he turns to me, putting

his hand on my exposed leg. "Have I told you how beautiful and sexy you look tonight?"

"You have. About seven times, but thank you. I don't tire of hearing it. You're very good for my ego."

He moves his hand up a bit so that now it's partially under my skirt. I put my hand on top of his, silently letting him know that's it. No higher. He doesn't push it.

He's moving his thumb in circles on my thigh as we chat. Truth be told, it's turning me on. I'm not even sure he realizes that he's doing it anymore, but having not been touched for so long, the smallest amount of touch right now is doing things to me. Jackson touching me is doing things to me.

The Darian of years ago would have encouraged him to keep going. The current Darian knows this is our first date and I need to keep things moving slowly for my own sanity.

After about twenty minutes of talking, we begin to look at the menu. "What's good here? What do you normally get?"

"Honestly, the food isn't that great here. It's really all about the ambiance and the music."

"It's a good thing I'm not a foodie, and never really care about the food at all. As long as there are good drinks and good   company, I'm a happy woman." That's the truth. I could care less about food. Drinks and company are all that matter to me.

"That you shall have." At his suggestion, we order a few   appetizers to share and another round of drinks.

Despite needing at least one hand, sometimes two, for the food and drink, there is always a part of his body touching a part of mine. I'm finding it very distracting. Nonetheless, we manage to eat, drink and talk some more until the music starts. He's extremely easy to talk to.

The lights eventually go down, and the jazz band starts.

The music can best be described as sensual. I've never really been into jazz, but this place and the music are kind of sexy. It's very soothing. I can understand why he loves it here so much and why he finds it relaxing. We're really enjoying listening to the music. After a few songs, he leans over and starts to kiss my neck. That's my Achilles heel. I'm powerless against a man kissing my neck. It's always driven me wild. I tilt my head a bit to the side to give him better access. I can feel him smiling against my neck when I do.

He's got one arm around me, one hand on my

thigh, and his lips are moving up and down my neck. I'm on sensory overload.

I let it go on for a few minutes, but then I'm finding that I need more. I take my hand to his face and guide his lips toward mine. We kiss slowly and tenderly at first until we are full-on making out.

I couldn't tell you the last time I just made out in the middle of a public place. I'm so turned on. I seem to have completely lost control of myself and the fact that I'm sitting in a restaurant.

I must be out of my mind because I take my other hand and place it on his cock. He's hard as a rock, and it seems to be taking up an awful lot of space in his jeans. I start rubbing him. He moans and moves his hand further up my thigh. I'm completely lost in the moment. I spread my legs a few inches in invitation. He pulls away from our kiss and looks at me in the eyes, out of breath from our kiss. His stare is intense and his eyes are full of want.

I look around to see if anyone is watching, but it's so dark in here, no one can see under the table, and everyone's eyes seem to be on the musicians anyway.

He keeps moving his hand up my thigh until he reaches my lace underwear and pulls it to the side. He sweeps his fingers through my drenched lips and I nearly buck off of my seat. I'm going out of my mind.

He slowly slips a finger inside of me. I lean my head back against my seat. It's been so long since anyone was inside of me. It feels so good. I close my eyes and moan. He takes that as a green light to start slowly pumping his finger in and out of me.

He whispers in my ear. "You're so tight. And soft. And wet." His words and hands have me two seconds away from coming. He slips in another finger and then rubs his thumb around my clit.

That's it. Game over. I erupt pulsing around his fingers. It feels amazing. He kisses away my moans, otherwise, I may very well have been louder than the musicians. That was embarrassingly quick.

When I eventually come down from my orgasm coma, he breaks our kiss, pulls his fingers out, and goes to put them in his mouth. I grab his wrist and bring his fingers to my mouth and slowly suck them as I stare into his eyes.

His eyes are completely filled with lust. After I finish sucking his fingers, I kiss him so he can taste me. His eyes practically roll to the back of his head. "We need to get the fuck out of here." He reaches into his wallet, throws down a few hundred dollar bills, grabs my hand, pulls me up, and we quickly exit the restaurant.

The car ride back to my house is quiet. It starts off sexually charged, but as we get closer, my senses begin to return.

I let this go too far. What was I thinking? I can't do this. Going any further may be a mistake. I feel bad, but I've been clear with him with regard to my reservations over dating him, and my need to take things slowly. He'll have to understand.

While I get that he is a man and has needs, especially after what we just did, to his core he is a good man and will   understand. I know that.

We pull up to the house and he parks in my driveway. He gets out and opens the door for me, gently grabbing for my hand and kissing it.

I open the front door slightly and turn to him. "Jackson, I'm so sorry but I need to slow things down. I should not have let things go as far as they did back there. I'm incredibly attracted to you and got carried away. I can easily see you coming inside. Believe me, I can see you coming inside. But this is our first date. Hell, this is my first date with a new man in twenty-eight years. My mind is just all over the place. I apologize that I led you on and let it go so far. I understand if you're upset with me. And while..." He puts his finger over my lips.

"You're rambling. You don't need to apologize,

sugar. You   control the pace. I told you that from day one. I completely understand. I always want you to be comfortable." He tucks a few strands of my hair behind my ear and rubs my cheek with his thumb.

"Can I just make one counter-argument, counselor?" I bite my lip to unsuccessfully attempt to hide my smile and nod.

He begins, "I reject your notion that this is our first date. Did we not sit at a bar last Friday, have a drink, and talk? In my book, that's the very definition of a date." I slowly nod.

"Did we not talk for hours each night for six nights? While perhaps that doesn't fit into the strict dictionary meaning of a date, it's a slippery slope and there's most definitely an   argument to be made that each night spending hours speaking with one another can each individually be considered a   separate date." Fucker. I smile.

"And last night, while we were together briefly, there was a rather passionate kiss, and I would argue that it should count as a date as well. So, by my math, this could very well be considered our ninth date. I therefore conclude that you should feel as comfortable as you would if this was our ninth date. Whatever that may be." He finishes with the biggest smile I've seen to date.

He's so good-looking. Even more so with that smile. He's so close and he smells so damn good. I'm silent for a few moments. He does make some compelling arguments.

My eyes are looking everywhere except at him. I know if I look into those emeralds, I'm a goner. The bastard knows it too. He gently takes my chin and brings my eyes to his. He lifts his eyebrows waiting for an answer.

I must still be drunk on my orgasm, because the next thing I know, I say something along the lines that he should have been a lawyer, I grab him by the lapels of his jacket, pull him towards me, and crash my mouth onto his.

The kiss goes from zero to one hundred in about three seconds flat. He picks up my legs and wraps them around him. With his foot, he closes the door behind us. He breaks our kiss and moves down to my neck, murmuring for me to point to my bedroom. I point as I start to rain kisses on his neck. He tastes good.

We kiss for a few more moments as he walks us through the house, with me wrapped around him. He's such a good kisser. His big, juicy lips are made for kissing.

He eventually sets my feet down on the ground near my bed and slowly removes my sweater, in complete contradiction to the frantic pace of our kisses just moments ago.

He expertly undoes my bra and it falls to the ground. His eyes roam my breasts as if he's committing them to memory.

He's then on me kissing me again, slowly this time, as he tenderly grabs my breasts. He smiles into my mouth whispering, "yes real, and yes spectacular." I smile back into our kiss as I remove his blazer and unbutton his shirt. When I remove his shirt, I look down. He is ripped and sexy as hell. Broad chest. Six pack. Black hair across his chest, and another trail of black hair from his belly button through into his pants. I take a step back and stare. "You look like you were photoshopped."

He laughs briefly but turns serious again. "I really want to fuck you in that skirt. I've been imagining it all night. I will in the future, but right now I need to see your whole beautiful body."

I'm all of a sudden feeling very self-conscious. I'm forty-eight years old and I've had three kids. While I'm in reasonably good shape and have a pretty good body, I don't have the body of a twenty-five-year-old Adonis like he seems to.

He unzips my skirt and lets it drop to the ground. He slips his fingers into the top of my lace thong and slowly moves it down my legs. He kisses a trail along my legs and body on his way back up, finishing with a tender kiss on my lips.

He takes a step back and really looks at me. "You are the sexiest woman I have ever seen in my life."

That settles my nerves and gives me the confidence to step forward, press my chest to his, and kiss him again while I undo his belt, button and zipper. I slide his pants, along with his boxer briefs, slowly down his legs.

Just as he did to me, I kiss my way up and finish on his lips. I take a step back toward my bed so I can really see his gorgeous body. He has thick, muscular quads. As I get my first look at his cock, my eyes almost pop out of my head. He wasn't kidding on the phone. That is the biggest damn cock I have ever seen. That sucker may split me in half. I can't wait to find out. He smiles knowingly.

He walks towards me and slowly lays me down on the bed, positioning himself on top of me between my legs. He rubs one of my breasts while he licks and sucks the other.

He stops and looks up at me, "you realize that every woman on this planet would kill for these perfect tits." I smile as I thread my fingers through his hair while he continues his licking and sucking, finishing with one breast and moving to the other, giving it the same delicious attention.

I'm writhing beneath him. He then moves up to kiss me. He really likes kissing, and I really like kissing him. I can feel his cock sliding between my legs and I may have another orgasm from just this.

It starts to become too much. I'm impossibly turned on.   "Jackson, I need you inside of me."

"I need to taste you first. The leftovers at the restaurant didn't quench my thirst for you."

He kisses his way down my body until his face is between my legs. He spreads my lips and takes one long, slow lick. He closes his eyes and mutters "yum."

It's so intimate, and it feels so damn good. I need more. Much more. I grab his hair to guide him back down. One lick wasn't enough for me.

He smiles into me and then buries his face licking and   sucking me. He is really good at this. It's going to take me all of thirty seconds to come again. He brings one hand up and plays with my nipples while he continues licking me. Squeezing my   nipple is a direct line to my clit and I moan out in pleasure. I'm already teetering on the edge.

He's alternating between licking and sucking on my clit. The dual sensation is sending me over that edge. I'm almost there.

He slowly moves his hand back down my body and slips two fingers inside of me. The pleasure overtakes my senses. "Oh God, Jackson. That feels so good." He pushes all the way in and starts slowly pumping, going deep each time, finding that exact right spot.

After only four or five pumps, my body explodes into orgasm as I scream his name. He lets me ride out the orgasm, and doesn't stop until I grab his face and pull it up towards mine.

I kiss him passionately, tasting myself on him. We kiss and kiss while he slides his cock through my drenched, sensitive lips.

I go to move my body down his, dying to taste him too, but he keeps me up and says "no, I need to be inside that perfect tight pussy right now." I spread my legs more in invitation.

He slowly enters me. Inch by glorious inch. It has been so long for me. This feels so good.
I think I almost forgot how amazing sex feels. I can feel my body relax and my legs start to numb with pleasure.

He eventually gets his monster cock all the way inside of me. It takes a few seconds for me to acclimate to his size. He understands and pauses inside of me, looking at me with such lust and passion.

He brings his hand up and gently caresses my face looking at me in the eyes. "Darian, you feel like heaven." I close my eyes. He kisses me and his tongue slips into my mouth as he begins to move inside of me.

My entire body is completely consumed by him and overcome with pleasure. I'm going to come again. I can feel it at the surface.

He continues to kiss me, increasing the passion of the kiss as he moves faster and faster inside of me. "Oh God, I can feel your walls pulsing around my dick. It feels so good."

They're about to pulse a lot more as I again orgasm screaming his name. He keeps pumping, seeing me all the way through my peak.

As I come down from my third orgasm of the night, he lifts one of my legs and really starts to pump into me. He's now   pounding me hard and fast. I don't know how he's lasting so long. Clearly, I don't have that ability. He's a machine.

He kisses down my neck as the pounding continues. He takes my nipple into his mouth and sucks hard. Oh God, here I go again, I'm pulsating into another orgasm and I can feel his control slipping as we come together, with me screaming and him grunting.

After a few moments of heavy breathing, he lets

go of my leg and kisses his way up from my chest to my lips, giving me one final deep kiss.

He rolls to the side and pulls me in close to him. He whispers "are you okay," as he peppers my face with kisses. Tears come to my eyes. "Don't cry, sugar. I'm so sorry. Was it too much too soon?"

I turn to him and smile as I softly kiss his lips. "I'm not crying for the reason you think I'm crying. I'm just being emotional over how considerate you are." And it's true.

"Thank you for taking care of me." I thought I would be freaking out about sleeping with a man who isn't my husband, but I'm not. I'm happy we did this. It was amazing. He's amazing. I'm happy it was him. He really did take such good care of me.

As I inevitably come down from my sex coma high, it all of a sudden it hits me. We didn't use protection. I haven't had to think about protection since my last child was born, and Scott had a vasectomy just after I gave birth. Using protection didn't even occur to me.

"Jackson, we didn't use a condom. I'm sorry. It didn't even cross my mind. I was so consumed with what we were doing, that I completely forgot. That's basically the bad excuse for every teen pregnancy." I'm so embarrassed.

He laughs hard. "Well, my boys always wanted a little sister." I look at him like he's crazy. I'm going to kill him.

"I'm just kidding. I had a vasectomy years ago and I haven't had sex with anyone in six months. Actually, any sex I've had since my divorce was with a condom, but that was for different reasons than preventing pregnancy. This is the first time I've had sex without a condom since I was married. I wasn't worried about you. I know you haven't had sex in three years. I forgot how good it feels to go bareback. Or perhaps it's just you that feels so good. That's definitely what it is." He turns and rubs his hand down my body.

I breathe out a sigh of relief. Phew. Add this to the list of things I haven't thought about in a hundred years.

"Are you really okay, sugar?"

"I'm really okay. I'm more than okay. That was incredible,   Jackson." I cup his face and kiss his lips.

He smiles. "For me too." He kisses me again.

After I go to the bathroom and clean up, I come back out and see him laying there in all his naked glory looking sleepy. He's definitely a vision to behold.

I'm not sure what's 'normal' here. Is he supposed to get up and leave? Is he supposed to stay over? Am I supposed to be the one to ask him to stay or leave? I kind of don't want him to leave. I'm enjoying my Jackson bubble and I'm not ready for it to pop quite yet. "Do you want to stay over?"

He smiles again. "I'd love nothing more than to hold you all night and wake up and do this all over again."

Sounds like a plan to me. I slip into bed and nuzzle into his big body. This simple intimacy feels so good after not having it for so long. I've missed sleeping cuddled up into a man's warm body. I particularly like Jackson's big arms. I lay my head on his chest. After four orgasms I'm exhausted and easily drift off to sleep.

CHAPTER 8

Harley

"Skylar, Jason is a dick. You need to be done with him once and for all. He treats you like shit. Trust me, I know what that's like to be ghosted. You're better than this."

"Why, what's going on with you? Did you meet someone?"

I'm definitely not ready to discuss this with her. "No, just friends with bad past experiences. You need to send this guy packing."

"Maybe. He doesn't treat me like shit. He's amazing when we're together. He just goes off the grid sometimes. But I agree, it's pretty sketchy."

"Damn right it's sketchy. If it wasn't sketchy, he'd tell you what he's doing. We can talk more about Jason tonight at dinner. I'm almost at Mom's house."

"No, we have no need to further discuss my love

life at dinner. I'd rather spend tonight asking Mom about her date last night. I'm so proud of her for going. Do you think she put out?"

I laugh. I didn't even think about that. That would be weird. My Mom getting intimate with a guy who isn't my dad. I'm happy she went out though. She's been sitting home miserable for three years. She's been alone for so long. I'm just thrilled she's doing something besides sitting at home.

"We'll definitely need details from Mom. I'm here. I'll let you know if I get anything good out of her. I'll see you later   tonight."

I end the call and pull into Mom's long driveway. As I get closer to the end, I see that there's a strange car there. A really   nice strange car. No fucking way. Does this belong to Mom's date? I will be officially living my dream if I get to return the favor and bust Mom with a boy in her bed. This would actually be   Reagan's dream. She got busted with boys in her bed more times than I can count.

I quickly hit the button on my cellphone to FaceTime Skylar. She answers right away. "Didn't we just get off the phone? Miss me already?"

"Yes, terribly. I thought you'd want to know that I just pulled into Mom's and there's a strange car in the driveway. Do you think her date from last night is still here?"

"Oh my God. This is amazing. Keep me on the phone. Make sure you're pointing the camera at them when you go inside. I want to see what goes down. Wait! Add Reagan to the call. She'll want to see this too." I quickly add her number to the call and it's ringing.

"What the fuck? This is my one day off. Why are you calling me so fucking early? And why are you FaceTiming? Is it 2012?"

"I'm at Mom's and I think her date's car is still in the driveway. Skylar and I want to bust her on video. We'd thought you'd want in on the action."

"I'm up! Can we record this too?" Skylar and I both laugh. "This could be epic."

"Don't talk. I'm going in quietly. I feel like a burglar." I'm also trying to hold two coffees. I enter the code into the keypad on the front door. It's completely quiet in the house. I place the coffees on the kitchen island and tip toe towards the bedroom. The door is open. I whisper, "there are definitely two bodies in the bed."

Skylar whispers, "keep going and turn the camera so we can see."

I suppose that could be Aunt Cass in bed with Mom. She sleeps with Mom all the time, but that's not her car. I'm tip-toeing further into her bedroom. I get a little closer. Nope, that's a big, manly body. Definitely not Aunt Cass. I turn the phone camera to my face and mouth "Oh. My. God." I turn it back so they can see what I'm looking at.

Reagan whispers, "get closer, so we can see them. I want to get a screenshot."

I manage to get right next to the bed undetected. All those years of terrible ballet classes have finally paid off.

I smile at what I find. As if it's Christmas morning, there's Mom, with some ridiculously hot, ripped older guy completely blanketing her. They're both naked. The sheets are pooled around their waists and they are asleep with both of his hands wrapped around her boobs.

Reagan and Skylar can't control themselves and bust out laughing. I see Mom's eyes start to flutter open. She croaks out, "Harley, is that you?"

I smirk. "Yes, Mom. Reagan and Skylar are here too." I show her the phone. "We all wanted to wish you a good morning. It   certainly looks like you had a good night."

Her eyes pop open and she looks down at her man hand covered boobs. "Oh shit. Jackson, wake up." She throws a bit of an elbow at him.
The man that I assume is Jackson stirs but

doesn't open his eyes. He just starts kissing her shoulders and back, while his hands become a bit more active on her boobs." Reagan and Skylar laugh louder, which seems to wake him up.

He smiles as he looks at Mom, but then his eyes move to me and his smile fades. "Um, hello?"

I have a big shit-eating grin on my face. "Hi. I'm Harley, Darian's daughter. So nice to meet you." I hold out my hand, fully smirking, while my sisters are belly laughing.

"Well, I'd shake your hand hello, but I feel like that would put your mother in a compromising position." Reagan and Skylar are fully cackling now.

"He's funny, Mom. I like him." I turn my eyes back to Jackson. "Jackson, this was a house of four women. If you think I haven't seen my mother's boobs thousands of times, you would be mistaken. I understand the appeal though." I wink at him.

"Oh my God! Harley, get out of my room! I'll be out in a few minutes. Why are you even here?"

"I came for Dad's letter."

"Oh, okay. Just give us a few minutes."

Reagan yells, "don't worry Mom, we got screenshots of this. We're having them made into posters for our rooms. Maybe it will even be our Christmas card this year." The three of us are in hysterics.

"Out!"

I exit the room and close the door behind me. The three of us continue laughing as we recount the events of the past five minutes.

Skylar calms down first. "That was fantastic. Send the pics in our group chat. Aunt Cass will want to see them too. We'll show them to her tonight."

Reagan chimes in, "thank you for waking me. This was the best morning of my life. Call us back after you talk to her. I can't wait for dinner. We're gonna torture her." We sure are. We say our goodbyes while I wait for Mom's walk of shame.

Darian

I turn in the bed toward Jackson and bury my head in his chest. "I'm so embarrassed. I'm really sorry Jackson."

"It's kind of funny. It definitely could have been worse."

"It is not funny, and I don't think it gets much worse."

"It could have been in about thirty minutes from now when you would have been in a much more compromising position." Oh. I feel my cheeks getting flushed. Now I'm thinking about doing that again, but I guess that's the last thing I need right now.

He squeezes me tightly. "I had a great time last night. I hope you did too."

I look up at him and smile. "I did." He softly kisses my lips. Resigned to the fact that there will be no morning fun, with one last kiss I roll out of bed and throw on my robe. I brush my teeth and grab a spare toothbrush for Jackson. He brushes his teeth and gets dressed as well.

He turns to me as he's finishing at the sink. "Hey, what did Harley mean when she said 'Dad's letter'?"

Jackson doesn't miss a thing. "Scott always assumed he would die young. His father and grandfather died of heart disease young too. I was in denial, but he never was and planned accordingly. He prepared letters that are to be given to the girls at various milestones in their lives. I have them locked up, and when they reach those milestones, they get their letters. They've received a few, like when Skylar and Reagan turned twenty-one, as well as Reagan and Harley's graduations. I have several still stored for more graduations, when they get married, when they have children and few other things. There's one for Harley for the day she officially became a doctor, and I know she's anxious to read it."

He smiles. "Wow, that's really nice for the girls. Do you get   letters too?"

"I only received the one he wrote for me right after he passed." I read that letter every day, but Jackson doesn't need to know that.

He thinks for a moment. "Do you get to read their letters?"

"They've let me read all of their letters except the first they each received after he passed. Whatever he wrote in those   letters, they didn't want me to see it and I respect their wishes. I'm sure it's about their responsibilities to take care of me and they don't want me to see it so I don't feel like I'm a burden to them."

Jackson hugs me. "He sounds like he was a good man."

I look up at him. "The best." I swallow back my emotions. I wonder if it's weird for him to talk about Scott. He's the one who started this conversation though. I'm just being honest.

After we finish washing up, we exit my bedroom and we walk out into the kitchen. Harley is sitting there sipping her coffee, still grinning. "I guess you two should officially meet. Harley, this is my friend Jackson Knight."

He sticks out his hand and they shake hands. "It's a pleasure to meet you. Happy to be able to shake your hand this time." She giggles. He smiles warmly at her. "You're a very lucky woman. You seem to have inherited your mother's good looks."

"Thank you. It's nice to meet you as well. I'm sorry, I didn't know you were here or I would have brought you a coffee as well. I'm not really accustomed to Mom having overnight visitors."

"Harley!" She laughs.

I turn to Jackson. "Jackson, take my coffee. I can make some for myself."

"No no. I will grab some on my way home. Walk me out?"

"Okay."

"Nice to meet you, Harley. I hope to see you again soon, perhaps with clothes on and under slightly different circumstances."

She and I both laugh. "Nice to meet you as well. I can't begin to tell you how happy I am that we met under these circumstances.

You've given my sisters and me endless ways to torture Mom."

He grins as he grabs for my hand, which is a little awkward in front of Harley, but I guess she saw a lot worse this morning.

We get to the front door and he puts his arms around me. "I like your daughter. Obviously, a stunner like her mother, but she has a good personality too. She'd get along well with Trevor. He loves jokes at my expense as well."

"My girls *all* love jokes at my expense. They're going to have a field day with me at dinner tonight. And Cassandra is coming too which will only add fuel to the fire."

He chuckles before pulling me closer and rubbing his hands up and down my back. "Can I call you later? I know you have   dinner. Maybe after that?"

"Of course, you can. I'd like that."

"I want to see you again this week. I actually have a Children's Hospital black-tie fundraiser this Friday night. Would you like to come with me? I'd love to show up with the hottest date in town. It's good for my top bachelor in Philadelphia status to be seen with beautiful women." He winks at me. I shake my head at his playfulness.

I haven't been to something like that in ages.

"That sounds like fun. Thanks for inviting me. Seeing you in a tux will give me spank bank material for a year."

He laughs. "You, Darian Lawrence, are refreshingly honest. And a little bit dirty. I like that about you." He grabs both of my cheeks and gently tilts my head up so he can bring his lips towards mine. He kisses me softly. Longer than a peck, but not open-mouthed with Harley nearby.

He turns to walk out. "Bye sugar. Talk to you later."

"Bye Jackson." I close the door and take a breath. This guy. He's making me feel things. Things I haven't felt in a long while.

I turn back towards the kitchen to the firing squad waiting for me. Here we go. Harley has one big smile on her face as she hands me my coffee. "Thanks. This feels like a walk of shame."

"It's not really a walk of shame if it's in your own house and you're in your own robe. Jackson going home in his clothes from the night before is a real walk of shame. But I guess your daughter coming in and seeing you naked with some strange guy's hands on your boobs is at least a partial walk of shame." Said as she smiles innocently.

"Thank you for the clarification," I add sarcastically. "I wouldn't want to get my walk of shame situations wrong." I sit down next to her and silently start in on my coffee.

"So, Mom? What's the story? Obviously, you liked him. You gave it up to him." I roll my eyes. She giggles. "He's really good-looking, even for an old guy."

"That he is. And he's not old. He's a year older than me. Anyone above thirty is old to you." I take a few more sips as I think.

"I don't know, babe. This is the first guy I've gone out with since Dad. In part, it feels weird to spend time with someone that's not your father, but it also feels nice to have someone again. It's been a lonely three years." She frowns at that.

I grab her hand. "You know what I mean. You girls have been amazing, as have Aunt Cass, Gennifer and Alexandra. You know it's a little different than spending time with a man. Jackson has been wonderful and understanding of some of my issues with moving on. I think we've been pretty honest and truthful with one another. I had a really nice time with him, and it's been a long time since I've had a nice time with a man." That's the plain and honest truth.

Harley hugs me with a layer of tears brewing in her eyes. "Well good, Mom. You deserve to be happy. You know Skylar, Reagan and I just want you to be happy. None of us want to see you sit at home by yourself every night. You're too young and too pretty to do nothing. We all want you to enjoy yourself." She's so sweet. I love my girls so much.

"Thanks, baby, but this is very new. We've only known each other a little over a week. We'll see what happens."

"I heard him ask you out again."

"Yes, he did. Thanks for eavesdropping."

"I also heard him kiss you," she smiles.

"He's very kissy and very touchy. It's actually kind of nice." It is nice. I've been kind of starved for affection, and Jackson is   extremely affectionate.

It's time to change topics. "Why don't I go and get your letter."

I go to our safe and grab the envelope that reads "For Dr.   Harley Madison Lawrence when she officially becomes a doctor". I already have tears in my eyes and I haven't even read it yet.

I bring it to her and she goes into one of the other rooms to read it by herself.

I decide to use this time to throw on some clothes. I head into my bedroom and find my cell phone on the floor. I must have dropped that in the shenanigans of last night.

I pick it up to see twenty-five missed text messages. Twenty-two are from our family group chat with Skylar and Reagan rehashing the details of this morning, along with a few screenshots.

I click off those without fully reading them. Although I do pull up one of the pictures. Oh my. He is really holding onto my boobs for dear life. We do look sweet and happy sleeping there together though. I may keep this one. I save it to my camera roll.

I scroll through more texts. There's a text from Cassandra late night last night asking about the date, and another from her this morning saying that she hopes my lack of response means what she thinks it means. I roll my eyes.

The last text is from Jackson from just a minute ago.

> Jackson: Missing you already. I can still smell you on my body. I may not shower for a few days. I don't think I can wait until Friday. Need to see you before then.

This guy is definitely intense. We did say we'd be straightforward and that we wouldn't play any games. I guess he's interested and putting it out there on the table.

I smell myself. I smell like him. It smells good.

I pick up the pillow he used and smell it. That smells like him too.

> *Me: You haven't been gone long enough to miss me. I can smell you on me too. I've got your smell on my pillow though, so I can take a shower. ;)*

I'm totally not showering right now. A few more hours of smelling like Jackson won't hurt.

I throw on some leggings and a sweatshirt and head back into the kitchen. Harley is just coming out of the guestroom with red eyes and tears streaming down her cheeks. "Oh baby, come here." I wrap my arms around her and hold her while she   finishes sobbing.

Eventually, she stops and pulls back. I look at the letter. "May I?" She nods. I sit down on the couch and take a big breath.

> *Dear Dr. Lawrence,*
>
> *I can't believe I get to call my first baby Dr. Lawrence. You are the first Lawrence in family history to become a   doctor. I've never been so proud in my entire life (and death if you're reading this).*
>
> *Harley, you becoming a doctor was never an if, but a when. You have wanted this since you were three years old. Your pre-school teachers even called us to say that while every other person in the class said they wanted to be something like a fireman, policeman, ballerina,*

or baseball player when they grew up, you were the only one to say you wanted to be a doctor.

Every picture you drew was of you as a doctor. Every Halloween for as long as I can remember, you dressed as a doctor. I keep a picture of you at 4 years old in a lab coat on my phone. Make sure your mom shows it to you today.

You have worked so hard and sacrificed so much throughout the years to make your dream a reality. Missed parties, dances, and games are just some of the sacrifices you made. No one has worked harder or deserves this more than you. Whatever specialty you choose, and whatever hospital you choose, they will be lucky to have you. I only regret that I can't be there to see you in your real lab coat at work. But I can imagine it, and baby, it's a thing of beauty.

Make sure you thank your beautiful mother for the sacrifices she made for you as well. You don't know half the stuff she did for you to lessen the burden and help you pave this path. She showed you every single day what a strong woman looks like, and we are all so blessed to have her as our family quarterback. Make sure you always take care of her and your little sisters. You four girls are my everything. Give mom a kiss from me. Tell her that I love her. I love you too.

Go get 'em, Dr. Lawrence!

My love always,
Dad

I am full-on sobbing now too. Oh, Scott. Why did you leave us? We miss you. We need you.

Harley sits down next to me and we both hold each other and cry. These letters from the grave are like a double-edged sword. It's so amazing to read new words from Scott, but at the same time, it brings so many emotions to the surface. Just when I think we're healing and moving forward, I realize we will never truly heal from losing the heart and soul of this family.

After thirty minutes of wallowing, I decide that we need to   soldier on. I get up and make us breakfast.

We chat about her new residency. She seems to really like it, even though it's difficult and the hours are insane. She said she doesn't have time to even think about dating, but I sense a story there. I decide not to push right now. She'll tell me when she's ready.

We talk for a long time and then watch a little mindless   Netflix together until it's already time to get dressed for our dinner. I shower and dress.

We head downtown and pick up Reagan on our way toward Skylar's school. Cassandra is meeting us there.

We meet everyone at the front of the restaurant and then all sit down. Cassandra throws me an elbow. "Thanks for returning my texts, bitch."

"I was with Harley today. She just got her doctor letter from Scott. It's been an emotional day." Cassandra nods knowingly and rubs my back with love.

Reagan immediately jumps into things. "That's not all Mom was doing today. Show Aunt Cass the photos, Skylar." Skylar is sitting next to Cassandra and shows her the morning photos. I'm just rolling my eyes and shaking my head.

Cassandra spits out her drink laughing. "Oh my God. Send me those. I may wallpaper my house with them." Cassandra and my girls are all laughing.

"Get your laughs out of your systems, ladies. I'm the one that had a hot guy in my bed this morning after an evening of   several orgasms."

Cassandra and Skylar at the same time both blurt "so did I," and then they all start laughing again.

They gossip and giggle about the morning for another twenty minutes until it finally mercifully ends.

Harley happily announces, "Jackson already

asked Mom out on another date. Some black-tie fundraiser on Friday. He said he was excited to have the hottest date there."

They're relentless. "You mind your own business, young lady." I flick her leg and she shrieks.

"Oh, you mean the Children's Hospital fundraiser. My firm is sponsoring a table. I'll be there too." Oh great, just what I need. Cassandra on my date with me. Who knows what will come out of her mouth. Well, at least I'll have a familiar face, if not a big mouth.

We chat and laugh and have fun, just like we do almost every Sunday night. These four ladies are my everything.

Reagan asks Skylar what's the latest with Jason. I can tell neither Reagan nor Harley like him. I haven't met him. A situation I clearly need to rectify. "I don't know. He's so hot and cold with me. One minute we can't get enough of each other, and the next he just falls off the grid for a day or two at a time and won't tell me what he's up to. I've never really been insecure in relationships, but this guy has my head spinning. We're not that serious. It's not a big deal. We've only been dating for a few months. Leave it be."

I hate hearing her like this. She's never like this.

Normally if a guy pisses her off, she just dumps him and moves on to the next. She's never insecure in relationships. I love that about her.

"Skylar, you are a smart, confident, beautiful woman with everything in the world going for you. You deserve someone who makes you feel good all of the time. Not someone who makes you feel bad half of the time. You're about to take your grad school boards and apply to business school. You don't need someone messing with your head and dragging you down."

"Yea, well the sex is amazing, so I'm not quite ready to give him up just yet. Maybe I'll keep him around for the last year of school and then cut him loose. I know you guys are just trying to help, but I really can manage this myself. I'm not exactly a doormat here." People have always thought it weird that my girls and I speak so openly about sex, but that's just how it's always been. Even when they were teenagers. I was always honest and open with them, and eventually, they became the same with me.

Scott and I always felt that showing the girls a healthy   relationship was a really important part of parenting, as was the ability to openly discuss things, and talk things through without fear of punishment. At times, our family dinners   included condom demonstrations, boyfriend intimacy information, and birth control pill instruction. Sometimes Scott would excuse himself if it became too much, but that's just how things were for our family. It makes me happy that the openness continues into today.

That all being said, I've always hoped that the open way we are, and the marriage they saw, would be conducive to the girls being in healthy relationships. It doesn't sound like Skylar is in one, and I don't like it at all. I will make it a point to come down and meet her for lunch soon to discuss things further. For now, I will respect her wishes and drop it.

Eventually, the girls head to the bar for their weekly sister time, also known as lemon drop shots, leaving Cassandra and me alone. The second they're out of earshot, Cassandra turns to me, "several orgasms? Details please."

"Oh, Cass. It was kind of a wild night, and he's a really   passionate guy." I go into full detail about the evening, from our under-the-table escapades at the restaurant, to my initial hesitation about sleeping with him, to the amazing sex we had.

"At least he knows what's he's doing. You never really dated anyone but Scott, but a man who knows what he's doing in bed is like a unicorn. You seem to have found two of them. I hate you for that." I laugh.

"I think you've found more than two men who know how to please you, Cass."

"Yea, but I'm running at like a 15-20% success rate. You're at 100%." I guess I am. I'm a lucky girl. I smile.

I decide to have some fun of my own and really make her   jealous. "He's hung like a fucking horse. I've never seen   anything like it. I wasn't even sure if I could take it all in. I thought he'd split me in half."

She glares at me while I smirk. "I have half a mind to throw this drink in your face. You better be lying." I shake my head no while continuing to smirk. "You are the worst friend I've ever had. I hate you. We're breaking up."

"You can never break up with me. You're stuck with me for life. I love you." I hug her and kiss her cheek. I do love her.

"I love you too and I'm happy for you. You deserve lots and lots of happiness, and you really deserve lots and lots orgasms." I giggle. "What now?"

"I don't know. He texted me this afternoon about missing me. It sounds like we're going out again on Friday. I'll see where it goes."

She smiles. "I'm so proud of you. I want my best

friend back and this is a giant first step in that direction. This is the first time I've seen her in a while. I love seeing this smile on your face. It hasn't left all night." I suppose she's right. I am smiling a lot tonight. Of course, it has a lot to do with being with my favorite four ladies, but I think Mr. Knight also has something to do with it.

We eventually say our goodbyes and I head home. I see that Jackson called while I was at dinner. I'm still a little emotional over that letter and trying to figure out what I want from this relationship. I text him letting him know that dinner ran late and that I'm exhausted, and headed to bed. I'll talk to him tomorrow. I think I fall asleep before my head hits the pillow.

CHAPTER 9

Jackson

I head into the office on Monday morning as a reenergized man. Saturday night was the best time I've had in years. Maybe even longer than years. I really like this woman. She's gorgeous, with a body that has me adjusting my pants every time I look at it. She's smart, funny, into sports, and even a little dirty at times. She's the full package. I give Donna an admittedly overenergetic good morning. She looks at me a bit skeptically, due to my particularly good mood.

After thinking better of asking me about it, she informs me that William left a message this morning and for me to please call him. I hope everything is okay with them. It's pretty early in Colorado for him to have already called me. I dial his number as soon as I sit down at my desk.

He picks up immediately. "Hey, Jackson."

"Hey Will. Is everything okay? Is everything good with Frankie and the kids?

"Yea yea. They're all fine. So, funny story for you. My kids started school yesterday and you'll never believe what   happened?" Whoops, I know where this is going. "They each received a brand new MacBook laptop from an anonymous donor. You wouldn't know anything about that, would you?

Busted. "Umm…nope."

"Liar!"

"Will, I'm just trying to support the kids in their dreams. I know things are tight. The twins just started college, and the rest are in high school with college on the horizon.   Having five kids isn't cheap. I'm just trying to help you out wherever I can."

"And you think donating to their college fund each and every year since they were born wasn't enough?"

"Just seeing to it that my investments are well protected. It's a sound business move to provide them with the technology needed to be successful." At least that earns me a chuckle.

"Jackson, I know I don't make the big bucks like you, but I'm a proud man and can pay for my own kids. I can buy them computers for school."

"I know you can, Will, but I just want to relieve some of the pressure. Why do I even work as hard as I do if I can't take care of the people I love." I can tell he's a little choked up, so I change tactics. "Besides, I need to alleviate some future guilt for when I steal Frankie away from you."

"Watch it, buddy. It'll ever happen. I'm too good in bed for her to ever leave me for the likes of a soft dick rookie like you." We both laugh at that. "How are your boys doing?"

"They're doing great. Trevor and Hayden are working hard in grad school. I haven't seen them much lately with all their studying, but I am seeing them today for lunch. Having   Payton run the business with me, and work by my side every day is my dream come true. He's getting really good at analyzing deals. He's definitely got the head for this business. Personally, he's in newlywed bliss right now with Kylie. They seem very much in love, and I couldn't be any   happier for him."

"Ah, I remember the honeymoon phase. We couldn't get enough of each other." I don't remember any such phase. That's because I never had it. I had newlywed worry that I had no money, no job, I needed to finish college, and my nineteen-year-old wife was pregnant.

William knows what my silence means. He changes the subject. "Are you seeing anyone?"

"Actually, I met someone."

"Really!?" He's shocked because I've never once mentioned anyone I'm dating to him.

"Yes. It's very new, but she's special. I'm really enjoying my time with her."

"Wow. I'm so happy for you. When can we meet her?"

"Let's not get ahead of ourselves. Like I said, it's new. Let's see how things progress before I think about bringing her home."

"Okay. Maybe over the holidays?"

"Maybe. I'll keep you updated." We've been together a little over a week and I'm already talking about bringing her home for the holidays. What the hell am I thinking? "I've got to get some work done, Will. Give my love to Frankie and the kids."

"I'll give it to the kids," he grumbles.

A laugh. "Okay. Bye Will."

"Bye Dick."

As soon as I hang up the phone, Donna comes

flying in. "You met someone? I knew that smile this morning meant   something."

"You need to stop listening to my calls. I run a large   business, Donna. I'm not going to sit here and gossip with you about my love life." She waves me away with her hand as if I'm speaking nonsense.

Just then Payton walks into my office. Donna turns to him. "Did you know your father met someone?" Shit. Here we go.

He looks back and forth between me and Donna. "For real? Who? What? When? Where? How?"

I ignore him. "Have you spoken with Abelson? I'm a week behind on everything, having been in New York last week hatching out the Pfeiffer deal."

"Nice deflection. We have lunch today with Trevor and   Hayden. We'll get it out of you then. Yes, I spoke with   Abelson early last week. He's good with our counter-proposal. He'd agree to just about anything to get our money. Once I sniffed that out, I threw in a couple of more favorable clauses for us. I just want to make sure we're completely protected and have as much control as possible. The lawyers have already drafted everything. It's sitting on your desk for your final review and sign-off."

"Good. I'm not going to review it. This is your baby, Payton. I want you steering the ship on this project. If you're happy with the contract, it's a done deal. I don't need to review it." He has a big grin on his face. This is the first time I've given him this type of control, with zero input or interference from me.

"Whoever she is, I like what she's done to your mood." He chuckles and leaves my office. She does do good things to my mood. I take out my phone to text her.

> *Me: Hope you had a great dinner with your girls. Now it's time for a dinner with your boy.*

She responds right away.

> *Darian: You're very presumptuous to assume you're my boy. I'd rather call you my man anyway. You, Mr. Knight, are all man.*

And just like that, I'm adjusting my pants. She really has quite the effect on me.

> *Me: Thanks to that comment, my manhood just grew. In the middle of my office. Thank you for that.*

> *Darian: Quite a sight, no doubt. I can't walk properly*
> *thanks to that manhood.*

She's killing me. I need to see her.

> *Me: When can I see you?*

> *Darian: Didn't we make plans for Friday night?*

> *Me: That's a lot of days away. I'm already suffering from*
> *Darian withdrawal.*

> *Darian: Don't be such a girl. ;) How about I make you*
> *dinner tomorrow night?*

> *Me: Deal. Have a good day. Be sure to ice to prepare for*
> *Tuesday.*

> *Darian: On it.*

I have a pretty normal, busy morning. I'm looking forward to lunch with all of my boys. It doesn't happen more than twice a month now that school is back in session.

We meet at a local sushi bar on campus in between classes for Trevor and Hayden. We all man hug hello. It's always so good to see my boys. They've grown up so much in the past few years. The twins look like men now. Trevor is the only one that looks like me, with dark hair and green eyes. Payton and Hayden look more like their mother, with blonde hair and blue eyes. They're all tall and handsome. I'm so proud of them and the incredible men they have become.

"So, how's school going for you both?"

Hayden chimes in first. "It's really hard. There's so much memorization of body parts and bones. It's kicking my ass right now. I can't keep it all straight."

"That's because he's never seen all of the female body parts, so he doesn't know any of them." We all chuckle at Trevor's response.

"Business school is fine. Living with you my whole life more than prepared me. Though if real-life experience helps, it sounds like I would have been pretty good at medical school too. Better than Hayden." He blows a kiss at Hayden, followed by Hayden giving him a dead arm punch.

"Boys, relax. Hayden, medical school will get easier. You take the toughest classes your first year. At least that's what I've heard. Stay focused. It will all be worth it. How's your mother doing?"

Hayden sees her the most. They're very close. "She's good. She keeps busy. She's seeing someone, but he's kind of a douche bag. I think he likes her money more than he   actually likes her. He seems to be enjoying an uptick in his new lifestyle."

"Keep an eye on her. All of you. Your mother needs you to protect her always. No one will love her like you guys do. I'll give her a call and check-in." I make a note to call her. The boys don't know it, but her money is protected from all future boyfriends, and husbands for that matter. She's too kind and trusting, so I made sure protecting her money from sleazeballs was part of our divorce agreement.   Everything is in a trust for her, so would-be sleazeballs can't touch it.

Payton smirks at me. "Speaking of seeing someone, Dad is seeing someone too." Trevor and Hayden's eyes pop wide open in surprise.

Trevor mumbles, "I thought Dad was asexual." Payton and Hayden laugh.

"Very funny wise guy. Just because you've never met   anyone, doesn't mean I don't date. I date. I just haven't met anyone I truly like until now."

"So you really like her? What does she look like?" Trevor only cares about one thing.

"She's stunning. And if you care, she's smart and funny too."

"We'll be the judge of that."

"Not if I can help it."

Payton, always the sensible one, asks "not to be a dick Dad, but are you sure she's with you for the right reasons? Obviously, you're an awesome guy and I suppose reasonably good-looking, despite looking like Trevor, but having money puts you in a weird spot in that regard. Your net worth is public information."

"She doesn't care about money. She didn't even know   anything about me the first week we were talking. We haven't really discussed it, but from what I can tell, I think she has money anyway. She has a really nice house. She's a successful attorney who runs her own practice. She's a widow, so there's no divorce situation there."

"A widow? Is she 80?"

"No, Trevor, you can be a widow before you're 80. I guess it's good you didn't go to medical school. She's 48. Actually   Hayden, her daughter just finished medical school here."

"Really? What's her name?"

"Harley Lawrence. I guess now it's Dr. Harley Lawrence."

"No shit? I don't know her, but I've definitely

heard of her."

"Really? What did you hear about her?" I hope it's good.

"Apparently, it's kind of not normal to both look like a   lingerie model and be the number one student in your medical school class at the best medical school in the country. At a minimum, that cements full legend status, and that is definitely her reputation at the school."

I smile at that. "Yep, that's her. I didn't know she was   number one in her class, but she's very attractive. She looks just like her mother." I wink at them. "I met Harley   yesterday. She has a really good sense of humor too."

"Model hot and is a doctor? Sounds like something I could work with. Can I get a fix-up, Dad?"

"No Trevor, you can't."

Payton jumps in to end the nonsense. "Well Dad, if you're happy we're happy. None of us are dumb enough to think you and Mom had a good marriage. You deserve a good   relationship and some happiness. I hope it works out."

Payton is always the sensitive and sensible one. It makes me sad that Melissa and I couldn't even fake our way enough to make our kids believe we were happy. I don't think either of us was terribly unhappy, we just weren't in love. We respected and cared for one another, but it wasn't what a marriage should be. It was more of a friendship. I'm sad that we didn't set a good example for my sons. I hope we didn't screw them up. I'm happy that Payton seems to be very much in love with Kylie, and Kylie with him.

"Thanks, Payton. I appreciate it. How's Kylie? When does she leave for her trip?"

"She's good. She leaves on Thursday for her cruise. Kind of her last hurrah with her girlfriends."

"What does that mean?"

He smiles and proudly announces, "when she gets home, we're going to start trying for a baby." Our table breaks out in cheers and congratulations. I couldn't be more excited.

"Congrats son. That's awesome. I'm so happy for you. I can't wait to be a GILF." Trevor laughs loudly and Hayden looks like he has no clue what I'm talking about.

Trevor turns to Hayden. "I can't believe we shared a womb. It makes a lot of sense that we're not identical twins. GILF is Grandfather I'd Like to Fuck. The real term is MILF. Mom I'd Like to Fuck. It's what you call hot moms. Get a clue, dude. Get your nose out of the books sometimes." Another punch to the arm ensues.

I turn to Payton as Trevor and Hayden continue to bicker and hit one another. "I hope you have a girl." He and I both laugh. "And for Christ's sake, make sure Kylie doesn't come back from that cruise with botulism. Those disgusting cruises are cesspools."

My strong dislike of cruises has been passed along to my kids. "I know. Why do you think I'm not going and why I refused to go on a cruise during our honeymoon. I don't get why she likes them so much. My kids are never going on a cruise." Agree.

Hayden and Trevor need to get back to class so they head out. Payton and I go back to the office.

CHAPTER 10

Darian

"Hey, baby. Harley read your doctor letter this week. It was so sweet and so special. She cried. I cried too. Thank you for providing them with these letters. They are incredibly special to all of us. It's amazing to get new words from you once in a while. It makes us all feel like we are still close to you."

"So... I met someone. His name is Jackson. Umm...well...we've been intimate. It was weird being with someone that isn't you. Not bad weird or anything. Just different. It's been so long since I was with anyone else. I hope you're not upset. If there was to be some thunder right now, I would understand." I   cautiously look up. Nothing. Phew.

"I guess you're okay with it. Anyway, he's really nice. The girls are all happy that I'm not sitting home by myself as much. They don't want me to be alone anymore. Honestly, Scott, I don't want to be alone anymore. I hope you understand. It doesn't change anything about my deep love for you. You are my forever. Bye baby. I love you always. I'll see you next Friday."

I ended up not seeing Jackson at all this week. He had an emergency situation with his New York deal and had to head there on Tuesday afternoon.

He sent me tulips every day in apology. I told him it wasn't   necessary, but he wouldn't listen. He felt terrible.

He isn't getting back until this afternoon. It was probably for the best. My head has been back and forth all week. At times I'm excited about Jackson, and then other times I have moments of guilt for being so interested in a man that isn't my husband. I eventually decided that I want to see where this goes. I meant what I said to Scott. I don't want to be alone.

Though it's not just about my loneliness. It's Jackson. I'm   incredibly attracted to him. He makes me feel good. He makes me laugh. He makes me happy. I genuinely can't wait to see him tonight.

He texted me that he hired a limo service so we can have a relaxing drink and talk on the ride into town. He also told me to bring an overnight bag so I can stay over at his place. After a bit of back and forth, I agreed.

I spent the afternoon primping, getting my nails, hair and make-up done with Cassandra. She promised to behave herself tonight. That would be a first. I'll believe it when I see it. I'm wearing a long spaghetti strap red dress, with a plunging neckline, and a high slit up the side. I look pretty good.

Jackson rings the bell at 7:00 on the nose. I open the door and before me is my very own James Bond. Holy hell. Jackson Knight in a tuxedo can simply be described as orgasmic. I'm speechless. I've never seen anything so perfect in my life. I feel my cheeks flushing.

He looks me up and down. I see his breathing become a bit more labored. He finally breaks the silence. "I'm speechless." My words exactly. "You are stunning. I've never seen anything so perfect."

He charges at me like a bull until my back is pressed against the wall in my foyer. He bends down and takes my lips in a searing kiss. It's just like our first kiss was, full of passion and need. His tongue enters my mouth. He is devouring me. I'm on fire.

Oh, this guy. He does things to my body. Eventually, we break apart, both completely out of breath. God damn he can kiss.

I look up at him. "Good to see you too. I'll be

right back. I need to go reapply my lipstick." And maybe change my underwear. I reapply my lipstick and bring him a tissue for his now red lipstick-covered lips. I wish he could leave it. It's kind of hot to see him marked as mine.

We're cleaned up and ready to go. He asks our limo driver to take some photos of us. We joke that it's like we're heading to prom.

I get in the limo and there's a Tito's with club soda waiting, along with a bucket of sliced limes. He's so thoughtful.

We each have a drink and talk the whole way down. Mostly about our respective weeks. When we arrive, he helps me out of the limo and takes my arm in his. We walk in and definitely garner some attention. They must be looking at 007 on my arm. I know I can't take my eyes off of him.

"Is Payton coming tonight? I'd love to meet him."

"Unfortunately, no. His wife Kylie is away, and he doesn't like to go to social events without her. I've gone to many of these dateless, and it does suck to be here alone."

That's kind of sweet that Payton only wants to go out with his wife. I can see the sweetness gene runs deep in this family. We head straight for the bar and he orders our drinks. I see   Cassandra immediately headed our way. Oh boy. This should be interesting.

She arrives and unashamedly looks me up and down. "Damn, Dare. You look hot. You could turn me." I shake my head. Here we go.

I squeeze her arm. She looks gorgeous as always. "You look hot too, babe, but not hot enough to turn me from that." I tilt my head towards Jackson.

"I saw what you walked in with. I don't blame you. Wow." She said that as if he couldn't hear her. She then gives him the full once over. She's shameless.

I roll my eyes. "I know you sort of met at Cover Me, but I don't think you two have formally been introduced. Cassandra Blackstone, please meet Jackson Knight. Jackson, this is Crazy Cassandra." I grin at her well-deserved nickname.

"Nice to meet you, Cassandra. I've heard *lots* about you."

"Oh really? Like what?"

"Nothing too crazy." He winks at me.

"Well, Jackson, I've heard that you've got a porn star dick." I choke on my drink. Oh my God. Fucking Cassandra. She   promised to behave tonight. It's been less than thirty seconds and she couldn't see it through. I'm mortified.

Jackson squeezes my hand in reassurance. He has a cocky smirk and replies, "and I've heard that you've got quite the porn collection."

Oh my God. Oh my God. Oh my God. This just got even worse. I can't believe he said that to her. She might actually hit me. We've been here for less than two minutes and it's already a disaster.

She looks at me with an expression that I can't read. "I think I like him. He can stay." Guess she didn't care as much as I thought. That or I'm going to get an earful later. Just then an attractive man comes over to our group and begins talking to Jackson. Cassandra mouths to me "he's hot."

Jackson pulls me close and introduces me. "Darian Lawrence, please meet Ethan Davenport. He's the CEO of Children's   Hospital. Darian is a corporate attorney. She runs her own   private practice." Ethan is tall with sandy-colored hair styled to perfection. He has big, warm brown eyes.

"It's   a   pleasure   to   meet   you,   Ethan. Congratulations on this event. It looks like a great success."

"Thank you. Yes, all the money we raise goes straight to the kids in need. Your friend Jackson here is a long-time   benefactor. We're very appreciative of all he does." I didn't realize that.

I'm proud of him. I'm in my Jackson haze when I feel an elbow from Cassandra. Ouch. That was unnecessarily hard.

"Ethan, please meet my friend Cassandra Blackstone. She's an M&A attorney with Cooper & Kronfeld."

"Ah, Cooper & Kronfeld also have a history of being extremely generous. It's a pleasure to meet you, Cassandra." He takes her hand and kisses it.

"The pleasure is all mine. How about you and I head over to the raw bar? I'm a big oyster fan." She doesn't really even wait for a reply. She loops her arm through his and pulls him towards the raw bar on the other side of the room that has more of a seating area.

"She's going to eat him alive," I tell Jackson.

"Actually, he's a bit of a playboy. He just plays it cool. I think he can handle her. Let's go find our table, sugar."

We make our way over to the table and everyone introduces themselves.

We eat our first and second course while making chit chat with the people at our table. We're having a nice time. Jackson is constantly touching me. He either has an arm around me or places his hand on my thigh under the table. A few times he has leaned over to kiss my cheek. I think he wants to make it known that I'm here with him tonight.

Jackson excuses himself to go get us more drinks, and a rather slovenly-looking man sits down in his seat. "Hey, beautiful. I'm Bryan. What's your name?"

This guy is kind of forward and annoying, but I don't want to be rude. "I'm Darian. It's nice to meet you. My date should be back shortly."

As if I didn't speak, and subtly let him know that I'm spoken for this evening, he asks me to dance. "No, I'm sorry. I'm here with someone else."

"Come on, just one dance." He goes to grab my elbow, but as soon as he does, he's lifted off of me by the back of his jacket and tossed a few feet"

"The lady said she's here with someone else." I see a fuming Jackson standing over the man.

"Fuck off Knight. She's too hot for you. I think she needs a real man."

Jackson practically growls. "I won't ask you again, Clarrett. Get the fuck away from her. In fact. Never come near her or speak to her ever again."

Jackson definitely knows and doesn't like this guy. He turns to me and calmly says, "*sweetpea*, would it be okay if Mr. Clarrett here never spoke with you again?"

"I'd be A okay with that, *honeybuns*." Jackson smirks at the equally silly term of endearment.

Bryan needs to get the last word. "You don't know what you're missing." He crudely grabs himself. "What I could do for you. To you." Who is this jerk? What adult acts this way?

I smile and slowly stand up, putting my arm around Jackson, snuggling into him. "Well Mr. Clarrett, I've got top-quality prime rib right here." I pull Jackson down for a searing kiss. "I'm not sure what would ever make you think I'd be okay downgrading to chicken McNuggets. Jackson, *honeybuns*, come dance with me."

Jackson and I both smile as we leave hand in hand and head out to the dancefloor. I hear Bryan calling me a bitch, but that just makes my smile grow even more.

We get to the dance floor and wrap ourselves around one another. Jackson smiles down at me. "Chicken McNuggets? Top-quality prime rib, huh?

"You bet. Grade A." I give his butt a little squeeze.

He puts his hands on my face and pulls me into a kiss. The kiss starts off sweet and tender but turns heated quickly.

We're completely in the moment and forget where we are. We are really going at it. His hands move to my ass and pull me in tight to his rock-solid erection. I start grabbing his hair, seconds away from mounting him, when I feel another hard elbow to my side. I pull from the kiss and see Cassandra standing there.

"Will you two quit it. It's like a porno out here. I'm normally all for it, but we're at a classy event and this shit doesn't fly."

Oh crap. I totally lost myself. So did Jackson. I hope we didn't have an audience. I take a quick peek around. It looks like we may have a few observers. Whoops. When Cassandra is the one telling you to chill out, you know it's bad.

We break away from one another and I tell Jackson that I'm going to the bathroom. I need to cool off. Cassandra comes with me. She grabs my arm. "Fuck that was hot. Any chance I can watch you guys later?"

"No Cass, you cannot watch me have sex with Jackson later."

"I basically just did. And it was smoking. Will you film it?" I give her a death stare and she laughs.

We get to the bathroom and I splash some cold water on my face. What is it about this guy? I lose my mind when I'm with him. "Dare, in thirty years of friendship, I've never seen you like this."

"What do you mean? Scott and I were always hot for each other."

"Yes, maybe in more private settings. Never all consuming, don't realize where you are, PDA like what I just witnessed."

Is that true? I guess it is. Scott didn't really like PDA. He'd hold my hand, hold his arm around me, or maybe even a few quick kisses, but never anything like what Jackson and I just did. I don't know what to make of it.

Cassandra makes eye contact with me in the mirror. "I can see your wheels spinning. Don't overthink this. Just enjoy it. Just do so a little more privately. You two are *fire* together. You're going to go home a fuck a horse-cocked supermodel tonight. Be in the moment and be thankful."

I take a long breath. "You're right. I know you are. I'm going to let myself have some fun. Jackson and I definitely have   amazing chemistry."

"That's the understatement of the year. Holy shit."

We walk out of the bathroom and Jackson is standing there with my purse. "I'm sorry if I embarrassed you, Darian. I'm just so attracted to you. I lose control around you."

He runs his hands through his hair. Cassandra disappears down the hallway, not needing to be here for this conversation. "In all honesty, I want you all the time. I can't stop thinking about it."

I grab his hands. "It's fine Jackson. I lost control too. We're both responsible." He brings my hand up to his mouth and kisses it. One finger at a time. I look up at him. He takes my breath away.

"I want you too Jackson." I press my hands and my chest into his chest and whisper into his ear, "right now." I grab his bottom lip into my mouth and suck it hard. When I pull my mouth away from his, his eyes pop open and he pulls out his phone and writes a text.

He looks back up at me. "I texted the limo driver. He's pulling around now. Let's get out of here." He grabs my hand and pulls me towards the front door.

We head outside just as the limo pulls up. Jackson tucks me into the limo, and then stands up and says something to the driver. All I hear is something about not opening the door.

I manage to close the privacy screen while he's talking to the driver. Jackson gets his big body into the limo.

As soon as the driver closes the door, it's like a starting pistol. We lunge for each other. We're kissing hard. It's all lips, tongue and teeth. Our hands are all over one another's bodies. I can't touch enough. I can't be touched enough. I need more.

Thanks to the slit in my dress, I can easily pull it up and   straddle him. I position myself on top of him, all while not breaking our kiss. I'm grinding onto his hard dick. I need some relief. Truth be told, I've been worked up for hours. Maybe days.

He pulls the top of my dress and my bra down freeing my breasts. He grabs them and buries his head in between them. He plays with my nipples. I moan. He moves his mouth down to my nipples and starts sucking on them. "Oh God, Jackson. You feel so good."

I'm grinding hard on him now. We're both completely out of control. I need more though.

I pull my knees around his and slide down the front of his body. I unbuckle his belt and unzip his pants freeing his   enormous, hard dick.

I lick the oozing precum off of his slit at the top and he sucks in his breath. I kiss and lick my way down. And it's a long way down. I suck his balls into my mouth and he groans. I slowly lick my way back up to the top and take him into my mouth. I can tell he's trying to maintain control but is about to lose it.

His dick is all the way in my mouth as I lick and

suck him. I'm squeezing his balls with one hand. With my other hand, I grab his hand and place it on my head, giving him permission to take control of my movements. If possible, that move makes him even harder.

He grabs my hair pushing my head up and down. I use my newly free hand and slip it into my own underwear. I'm so wet. I start to move in circles. I'm insanely turned on.

He's pushing my head down. I'm somehow able to open my throat and take him nearly all the way in. He's moaning. We're both teetering on the edge. After a few minutes, he pulls my head off.

"I need to be inside you." I climb back up and re-straddle my legs around him. He starts to pull my underwear to the side, but the lace is unforgiving. "I can't make enough space."

I look at him with a serious face. "Do what you've got to do, Jackson." He looks me straight in the eyes and tears my   underwear clear off my body as though it was a piece of paper. It may be the single hottest thing I've ever witnessed.

He slides his fingers through my lips. "You're soaking wet."

I look at him. "I have been since the minute I opened my front door tonight and saw you standing there."

He slips a finger inside me. I close my eyes. I can already feel myself clenching. I can tell he feels it too, as he makes an 'oh' with his mouth.

"Jackson, I'm about three pumps away from coming. Do you want it on your finger or your dick?"

He slowly slides his finger out of me, sticks it into his mouth, and sucks it, closing his eyes in pleasure. Damn, that's hot.

After he pulls it out of his mouth, he slowly kisses me. He goes from frantic to controlled. I don't know how he always   manages that, the slow and the fast. I'm not as strong.

I can't take it anymore. I go up on my knees, position him at my entrance, and slowly work my way down. Inch by gratifying inch.

Once he's all the way in, we sit still for a moment and let the feeling take over our bodies. I can feel the pleasure spreading down through my legs to my toes.

After enjoying those first few moments, I lift back up and then slam down hard. He grabs onto my breasts, playing with my nipples. It only takes a few pumps, but I feel myself start to pulsate meaning my orgasm is seconds away.

"I can feel you squeezing my dick." I can tell he's

trying to hold himself off. Lucky for me, I don't have to.

Just a few more times up and down on him, and then I feel the explosive orgasm rip through me, taking over my body.

At this point, my legs are completely numb. My toes are curled. My eyes must roll to the back of my head, because for a brief moment, I lose all visual ability, seeing only stars. Actually, more than a moment because the orgasm keeps going and going and going. I'm screaming his name and he's now sucking my nipples, further dragging on my orgasm.

I finally start to come down, but I know myself well enough to know there's another orgasm brewing in there. I'm still so turned on. My thirst for him has not been quenched.

Jackson lifts me up as if I weigh twenty pounds, which I don't, turns me around, and slams me back down hard onto his dick.

We're now facing the same direction. He has one hand still on my nipple playing with it, wraps the other arm around my waist, and starts moving me up and down.

I turn my head to the side back towards him and we kiss   passionately. He's slamming me up and down and it feels good. So good.

He takes the hand that was on my nipple and moves it down to my clit. He starts moving it in circles, consistent with the up and down movement of my body on his. I can feel myself heading over the edge again.

I'm so loud right now that I think people driving by can   probably hear me. Maybe even the people a town or two over. God knows what the limo driver must think.

Jackson grabs my waist even tighter. "Oh God, you're   squeezing around me again. It feels too good. I can't hold off anymore."

"Let go. I'm coming too." And he does. And I do. We jointly scream out in ecstasy. A few more pumps as we ride it out together.

Holy crap. That felt amazing.

It takes us a few minutes sitting there to regain awareness. We're both panting loudly. I lean the back of my head against his shoulder. He dots kisses all over my neck and cheek.

He eventually breaks the silence. "I think maybe we need to let this poor limo driver go home." We both laugh. I pull up his wrist and look at his watch.

"Oh my God. We must have arrived at your house more than thirty minutes ago. This poor guy has been sitting here   listening to me screaming bloody murder. I'm surprised he didn't check to see if you were murdering me."

"I told him under no circumstances was he to open the door when we arrived. We would come out when we were good and ready. He knew what was up."

"So you planned to seduce me in here, Knight?" I smile up at him.

"I think it's you who seduced me." He pulls my lips towards his and gives me one last deliciously wet, open-mouthed kiss.

We fix our clothing. There's nothing I can do about my just fucked hair and puffy red lips. Whatever. It's not like the limo driver doesn't know what was going on back here. He probably has a hazmat team on standby.

I look at Jackson's gorgeous face and whisper "ready for our joint walk of shame?" He smiles as he takes my hand and kisses it.

We exit the limo. Jackson grabs my bag and thanks the limo driver. I mumble a thanks, but I can't really look at him in the eyes.

For the first time, I look up and notice Jackson's house. Wow. It's gorgeous. It's big and modern. There are windows   everywhere.

There's not another house within sight. He must have over ten acres of land, though it's hard to tell at night. The house is sleek, exactly what I would expect from Jackson.

He opens the door and guides me inside. "Oh Jackson, this place is spectacular. I love it."

"I'm glad you like it. I actually spent a lot of time designing it with the architect. It's my sanctuary." I can tell he's proud.

"Well, you did an amazing job."

He spends the next fifteen minutes showing me around. It's an enormous open layout with high ceilings and exposed beams. It's decorated impeccably. He has a spacious gym and twenty-seat movie theater. With a little bit of lighting, I can make out the outdoor pool, and an outdoor kitchen and   barbecue area. It looks like there's a gigantic fire pit area next to it.

Lastly, he takes me into the master bedroom. It looks like it belongs in Architectural Digest. There's what must be a four-post California King bed. It's huge. There are more exposed beams, and giant skylights, with an extensive sitting area. It's simply perfect. He shows me his bathroom. The shower looks like it's built for ten people. I think I count eight various showerheads with two benches. But it's the bathtub that grabs my attention. I think you can definitely fit ten people in that sucker. "That's the best bathtub I've ever seen." I look at him hopefully.

He smiles at me. "Darian, would you like to take a bath with me?"

I jump up and down. "I would." He turns it on and throws in some bath salts and bubble makers. He also grabs us two towels.

I turn around for him to unzip my dress, which he does. He adds in a few wet kisses to my neck. I love when he does that.

My dress falls to the floor. As I only need to remove my bra, I say "you owe me a pair of fancy lace thongs, Knight."

"I'll buy you a hundred pairs if I can keep ripping them off you."

"Deal." I take a step into the tub and sit down. Heaven.

Jackson begins to undress. Actually, the tub isn't heaven. Watching him undress is heaven.

He hangs up his tuxedo, as well as my dress, and walks toward the tub, buck naked, in all his glory, with zero fucks to give.

He is the perfect male specimen. I've always been a chest person. I love a broad chest on a man. I love the way it feels and smells. There's just something so innately manly about it.

Jackson's chest is sexy as hell, but his quads are what really do it for me. They're incredibly thick and muscular. I can't take my eyes off of his quads. The gigantic cock laying between them doesn't hurt either.

I assume he's going to get in across from me, but he slips in behind me and pulls my body on top of his. I rest my head on his chest and shoulder, as he wraps his arms around me.

He moves his head down and kisses my cheek. We sit there in silence with our eyes closed for a few minutes, enjoying the warmth. He aimlessly strokes his fingers up and down my body.

I feel so content right now. He eventually breaks the silence. "You really can orgasm multiple times in rapid succession. It's amazing."

I giggle. "It's my greatest superpower," said while I bat my eyelashes at him. "You can get me three or four times in a row pretty quickly if you *really* work for it," I say in challenge.

"Challenge accepted." He takes a deep contented breath. "The way you squeeze me when you're about to come is like nothing I've ever felt. I may be addicted."

I choose not to tell him that I've heard that before. Instead, I go with, "I may be addicted to you as well, Knight." And that's the truth.

We sit in silence a bit longer when he shocks me with a   question about Scott. "Did you have a good marriage?"

I smile. "I had a great marriage. Scott was a wonderful   husband. It obviously didn't last as long as I would have liked, but I'm thankful for our twenty-five years together. I would have gladly taken twenty-five more if I could have."

"What made it great?" He looks at me in genuine wonder. "If you'd rather not talk about it, I understand."

"No, it's fine. It was great because not only did we deeply love each other, we liked each other. We enjoyed doing so many different things together. We made time for one another. I think when you have kids, people get so absorbed in them, that they forget about their spouse. They kind of stop working on their   marriage. That's when people start to grow apart. We never let that happen. If we wanted to go out, we got a babysitter. If we wanted time alone at home, the kids took a trip to the grandparents. We never took each other for granted and treated our marriage as something not to ever be neglected. And while Scott and I were not super PDA people, we were fairly affectionate at home. It makes me proud that our kids saw a happy, healthy, loving marriage. It's the kind I hope they have one day."

I can see him deep in thought over my words. He's made mention in the past over his marriage not having been great. Perhaps I shouldn't have said that last part. After a few moments, he eventually confesses, "besides the obvious things, that's my biggest fear as a parent."

I'm confused. "What is?"

"That my kids didn't see a happy, healthy, loving marriage to model themselves after. We always treated one another respectfully, we didn't really argue or anything, but there was nothing loving or affectionate about my marriage. We were a cliché of 'staying together for the sake of the kids'. We eventually were just two friends, cohabitating, raising kids. We peacefully co-existed with the only common interest being our love for our children. I don't want that for them. I want them to experience the real deal."

I kiss his neck and hold his hands in support. "At least it was peaceful. I've heard of much bigger nightmares than that. It's a lot worse for the kids when their parents aren't even on friendly terms. That's when it becomes toxic." I don't want to pry, but I do want to know more. "Was it physical?"

"At times, but that was based simply on basic human needs. Neither of us were the type to cheat, so when the need arose, we helped one another out with the release. There was no passion. I've had more passion with you the two times we've been together than in my entire marriage put together." That makes me sad. No one should live like that.

"While we had our physical needs, we didn't crave one another the way I crave you. Frankly, it's been a bit eye-opening for me. I'm starting to realize all that I've missed out on." He feels me tense up a bit at that comment.

"I'm sorry. I don't mean to freak you out. You and I discussed honesty and no games. I'm just laying it out there. I'm into you, Darian. I'm *really* into you. I understand your hesitancy, but I do believe on some level that you have similar feelings. I know you've had this same type of intimacy before, I just haven't and it's got me thinking about what I really want in life."

"Don't do that. Don't minimize what we have started here. Yes, I've had real intimacy before, but it's different because you and Scott are different. You are the same in that you're both good men, which is important to me, but different in most other ways. I like that. I'm not looking to find a carbon copy of what I had. You shouldn't want me to be looking to you for that. What we have is unique because it's between you and me. No one else." I take a breath in realization.

"I can admit that I'm feeling what you're feeling. You're not alone in this." That's very hard for me to admit to him, but it's true. There's something strong between us. I can't deny it.

He pulls my chin up and kisses me softly. "You're not just beauty. You're brains too."

I smile up at him. "With a good rack."

"With a great rack." He squeezes my breasts hard and I laugh. "I'm a little obsessed with this rack."

"So I've noticed." He bends his head down and starts kissing me. I grab onto those delicious quads that I'm seated between. Damn, they turn me on. They're so thick and hard, just like the rest of him.

He's still playing with my breasts. I can feel him harden into my back.

The kiss gets more heated, but then he suddenly breaks away leaving me panting and wanting more. I turn around to   straddle him but he stops me. "You, Darian Lawrence, are insatiable. Let's get out and dry off so I can properly worship your gorgeous body all night." Yes, please. Those are the last words spoken for a very long time.

CHAPTER 11

Jackson

I wake up in the morning to the sound of my coffee machine. I don't remember setting the timer, but I must have done it before I left for the evening.

I'm on my back naked, with my dream girl laying naked on top of me fast asleep. The sheets are resting just above her perfect ass. She's so beautiful.

Her head is laying on my chest, with her chest pressed against my stomach and her arms wrapped around me. Her body moves up and down with her steady breathing. I love the way she feels on me. She's so soft.

I feel myself getting aroused. This woman does things to me. I'm rubbing her hair and soft back, kissing her head, when I finally look up and see Trevor standing there   smiling. I slowly mouth "get the fuck out."

He puts his hands out with wide open palms

like he's   holding something big and mouths, "she has huge tits."

Now, I'm getting angry, and though I mean to mouth it, I clearly say loud enough to partially wake Darian, "out!"

With that, Darian stirs a bit. She must feel my arousal and takes it as an invitation to wiggle and start kissing her way down my body.

Trevor holds his stomach, bent over silently laughing. I tighten my arms around her to stop her downward progress. I was hoping Trevor would leave and she'd never know he was in here, but there's no stopping this now. "Darian, stop. We have company." Her eyes pop wide open. She starts to sit up but I hold her down, preventing her from exposing herself.

She then turns just her head to Trevor and then back up at me. She's smiling. Oh, thank God she's smiling. "Jackson, why does this keep happening to us? We both need better locks in our houses."

I laugh, as does Trevor. "True. Trevor, close the door and wait for us in the kitchen."

"Yes sir," he salutes and smirks.

She burrows her head into my chest. "Ugh Jackson. How much did he see?"

"Your body is facing down squeezed against mine. I don't think he saw any parts of your body that he shouldn't." I hesitate for a moment. "He may, however, have seen you start to head south on my body."

"Oh my God! That's even worse than him seeing me naked. He's gonna think I'm a ho."

"He's not gonna think you're a ho." I chuckle. "Knowing Trevor, he'll like you even more because of it. Come on, let's get up and get some clothes on. By the way, I really like where your mind was at when you woke up. Let's consider doing that again later." She smiles again and shakes her head.

I get out of bed but she stays in and moves all the way under the covers. "I'm sorry, but I can never leave this bedroom. I can't face Trevor. I'm afraid I'm moving into your bedroom. I'm now a prisoner in here."

"Sounds good to me." I flash a big smile at her. I brush my teeth and get dressed. Eventually, she does too. We head out into the kitchen. "Trevor, this is my good friend Darian Lawrence. Darian, this is my son Trevor."

"Nice to meet you, Mrs. Lawrence." Trevor shakes her hand.

"Nice to meet you too Trevor. I apologize for the

way we met. Ironically, your Dad met one of my girls in a similar fashion."

"Is that the hot doctor?" Darian snaps her head towards me. For fuck sake, Trevor.

I silently throw daggers at Trevor and then look at Darian. "Since Hayden attends the same medical school that Harley did, he knew of her reputation for being the top student in the class and mentioned it to us."

She looks at me knowing there is more to the story. "He may have also mentioned that he heard that she is extremely   attractive." I gulp. "I merely confirmed that she looks just like her mom." I gulp again.

Darian smiles. "Nice save, Knight." Trevor starts laughing at that.

"I like your personality, Mrs. Lawrence."

"Please call me Darian."

"I like your personality, Darian." He throws his head towards the coffee machine. "I made a pot of coffee. It should be ready by now."

"You made coffee for us? Then I like you too, Trevor. But maybe it's just because you look so much like your father, and I like him a lot."

She smiles playfully at Trevor, but I continue staring   daggers at him. "I don't. You are in the doghouse until you're fifty, Trevor." He laughs. He knows it's not true.

I pour three cups of coffee and we sit down at the table to chat for a bit.

"Trevor, your father tells me you want to eventually live in New York. How come?"

"I love Philly. I've lived here my whole life. I'm definitely a city boy. I love the fast-paced hustle and bustle of a city. And there's no better, no bigger, no more exciting city than New York City. It's just what I've wanted for as long as I can remember. I was really torn because part of me wanted to work for Dad, but there's always just been something   drawing me to New York City. I'm so grateful to Dad for   expanding his business into New York for me. He says it's not for me, that it's a natural progression for his business, but I know the score. He's doing it to keep his favorite kid happy."

I cough, "least favorite kid." We all laugh.

We sit and talk for another twenty minutes or so. Darian rinses out her coffee mug and says, "I'm going to head out, Jackson. I've got some things to do today. It was great to meet you, Trevor."

I stand up. "I'll drive you."

"No need. I ordered an Uber. It will be here in a

few minutes."

"You should have told me. I wanted to drive you home."

"I'm sorry. I wanted to give you some alone time with Trevor. I assumed his appearance meant you two had plans. I'm just going to grab my stuff. If you don't mind, I'm going to leave my dress hanging here for now. I've already added yet another walk of shame notch to my belt with Trevor walking in on us this morning. I don't need another with my Uber driver." Trevor laughs.

"Of course. Whatever you need. Maybe I can bring it by later. I'll walk you out."

I walk her outside. The Uber isn't here quite yet. I grab her into my arms and kiss her lips. "Another good night with you, sugar. And that was a first for me." She looks at me in question. "Limo sex. That was a first for me."

She smiles. "I may possibly have done that at my senior prom with my high-school boyfriend, but I can promise you that last night was *a lot* better. And my date last night was *a lot* hotter."

"And *a lot* more well-endowed."

She looks at me like I'm crazy. "Jackson, you're more well-endowed than anyone who has ever had sex in a limo in the history of the world. Probably even anyone who has ever even ridden in a limo or seen a limo or thought about a limo." We both laugh. She kisses me again.

"Well, it was number one on my fantasy 'to do' list, and you, my beautiful girl, more than fulfilled my fantasy."

"Ooh. Tell me more about this list. I'm game for checking off a few more boxes."

"I like your dirty streak and the way you think. I'm not sure. Maybe the whole naughty secretary bit in my office would be fun. I've never had sex in my office. Actually, why don't you compile a list and I'll make all of your fantasies come true."

We hear a noise and see the Uber pull in. She looks up at me. "Let me think about my list and get back to you." She reaches up and kisses me one last time. "I'll talk to you soon." She gets in the Uber and it pulls out.

I walk back into the house with what must be a big shit-   eating grin on my face. Trevor snaps me out of my trance. "Oh my God. You're such a girl. You're totally in lust."

"Shut up. You're a pain in my ass. Being as we didn't actually have plans, is there a reason you're here, other than to cock block me?

He laughs. "I totally did. Sorry."

"It's fine. I'm kidding. Sort of. Why *are* you here?"

"I ran into Bryan Clarrett's kid last night. You remember him? His name is Larry. He was on my little league team."

"Sure I do. I certainly know his dad. He's a jerk-off. In fact, he hit on Darian last night and she totally bitch slapped him."

"I love that, and we'll get back to her in a minute, but I need to tell you about Larry. I saw him at a bar last night. He was pretty tuned up. He was talking about how you fucked over his dad buying up some properties near their Megaplex, and now they're going to fuck you over. He didn't say how, or anything else, but he was dead serious. He was in a state of rage over it."

"Yea, Bryan called me a week or so ago ranting and raving about the Megaplex area buy-up. I actually acquired those properties to convert them into low-income housing that I'm planning to donate back to the city. He must have gotten wind of their intended use. At the time I acquired the group of properties, I didn't even know about the Megaplex. Driving down his property value is just an added bonus. It doesn't change my plans. The city needs the housing and those properties were thrown in with another deal. It's only costing me some renovation costs, which are tax-deductible anyway. Sucks for Clarrett's business, but this benefits so many needy families. I'm not changing course because he and his son throw a temper tantrum. I can handle those small-minded weasels."

"Okay good. I just wanted to tell you what I heard. I was worried." It's good to know my son has my back.

"Now back to your lady friend. One: She's totally hot. Nicely done." I nod in agreement.

"Two: If the hot doctor looks like her, you need to fix me up." I shake my head no. "I figured. Can't blame a guy for trying. Three: She's funny. Nice that she had a good sense of humor about this morning. It could have gone very wrong the other way."

"Yes, she's very funny. I love her sense of humor."

His eyes soften as he moves on with his list. "Four: Happiness looks good on you, Dad. I've never seen you like this with anyone, including Mom. I hope it works out for you guys." I get a little emotional at that. This is the first time my son has seen me in a happy relationship. It makes me proud. I hug him.

Darian

I ride home from Jackson's with a big smile on my face. I know it's cheesy, but he's kind of dreamy. I like how uncensored he is. It's nice. I also like that I got to help him fulfill the top fantasy item on his list. I'd like to do some more of that. It was hot as hell.

As we enter my driveway, I see Cassandra's car. I walk inside and announce, "honey, I'm home."

"In here with your coffee, sweet tits." I follow her voice to my family room. She's sitting on my couch watching TV. Nice of her to let herself in and make herself comfortable.

"There you are. Where have you been young lady? I was up all night worried sick about you." She smirks. "Oh, I know where you were. You were with James Bond getting fucked senseless. I'm so proud of you. All grown up and shit." We both laugh. She hands me my coffee.

"By the way, I got fucked senseless too. That Ethan guy acts all prim and proper, but he's a freak. And you know how much I dig freaks."

"Ooh. Tell me more."

"After the Hospital event ended, thanks for just leaving by the way, he took me to a voyeur club called Club Yeur."

"What does that mean?"

"It's a club where you can watch people fuck, be watched   fucking, or some combination thereof. We did all of the above. It was hot."

"Just when I think I'm adventurous, you come in and make me feel like a sixteen-year-old virgin."

"What did you do? When I left, he was all weepy and   apologetic about your porn show on the dance floor."

"It was not a porn show. We were just kissing."

"You were not just kissing. You were seconds away from being penetrated. Whatever. What did you do?"

"We fucked our brains out in the limo. It was really good. Then we took a bath together. Then we went at it again for half of the night. After two orgasms in the limo, I told him that I can often get up to three or four while having sex. He took it as a personal challenge and gave me five more."

"Seven orgasms last night?" I nod. "Wow. That's a great night. I don't think I could get that high."

"It's a gift. I'm very talented." I flash her a big overexaggerated smile. "How did you leave things this morning with Ethan?"

"This morning? I don't do sleepovers, babe. Since my last   divorce, the only person I've ever woken up to in the morning is you." She's so damaged. Getting screwed over by men her whole life has irrevocably damaged her. I'm sad for my friend, but she loves her life as it is. "After I grabbed my flash drive at the club last night, I high-tailed it out of there."

"Flash drive?"

"For an extra few bucks, they record you and give it to you on a flash drive. You know I couldn't resist that. Speaking of video recording, I can't believe you told him about my video collection."

I clench my face. "I'm sorry. It sort of slipped when he asked me why we call you 'Crazy Cassandra'. I feel terrible about it. I shouldn't have betrayed your trust like that. It was wrong."

"Whatever. I don't really care that much. It's forgotten." She's the best. "How are things otherwise with the dashing Mr. Knight?"

"Good. Really good. He's so loving and affectionate. The fact that he fucks like a beast doesn't hurt. He makes me feel good. And he's so open and honest. He kind of lays it all on the table. No games. He's made it clear that he's into me and wants to see me. I obviously have no dating experience, but it seems to me that someone so open is a bit unusual."

"I can promise you from firsthand experience that a man who is straightforward and honest is in fact unusual." She thinks for a moment. "Does this mean that my sex fiend nympho best friend Darian is back in town?"

"I think it might." We cheers our coffee cups.

"Thank God. I've missed her so much. I've been stuck hearing about vanilla sex from Alexandra and Gennifer for too long. I've missed your brand of chocolate." We both giggle at that. Just then we both get a text notification on our respective phones. It's our group chat with Gennifer and Alexandra:

> *Alexandra: It's official. My baby was conceived via blow job. I wonder if that's a first in history. I should call Guinness Book of Records and ask. I can't wait to tell my child about how they were conceived.*

Cassandra and I laugh. Only Alexandra.

> *Me: YAY!!! Congrats.*

> *Gennifer: Mazel Tov!*

> *Cassandra: My condolences.*

I give her a dirty stare. "Be nice."

> *Cassandra: And congratulations.*

Cassandra and I talk and nap all afternoon after our busy nights. When I wake up I have a text from Jackson that he wants to see me tonight. Cassandra said she has a date, so I don't feel bad kicking her out so Jackson can come over. He and I enjoy a bizarrely normal quiet night at my house, laying by the fireplace, watching a movie, and eventually enjoying each other's bodies.

CHAPTER 12

Darian

Sunday night dinner comes around with my girls and Cassandra. I pull Skylar aside as we're walking into the restaurant, and ask her to pick a date this week for me to meet her for lunch. She tells me that Tuesday works best for her. We arrange a time and place to meet near campus. I need to see what's going on with her and the man she's seeing. We all sit down and chit-chat for a bit about our various weeks. Cassandra recounts her awful date the night before.

Apparently, the guy thought it a good idea to tell Cassandra that his ex-wife left him because he couldn't get it up. Of all people to tell that to, Cassandra would have to be the least tolerant or understanding person.

"Can you imagine being on a date and within the first twenty minutes he tells you that he has a sexual dysfunction?" My girls and I are all hysterically laughing.

"I really didn't want to waste my time. Obviously, I knew the date was over right then. I was about to get up and leave but decided to stay and have a little fun with it. He didn't have a good personality about it though. At least own your shit. I spent the rest of our meal just fucking with him. I ordered a soft cheese platter to share with him. He didn't crack a smile. Then I suggested he order the softshell crabs or the softshell tacos. Again, nothing." The four of us are doubled over in a fit of laughter as Cassandra continues recapping the evening.

"After we finished the main course I asked him if he'd like to go for some soft-serve ice cream, that I knew where a Mr. Softee truck could be found. At that, he threw his napkin down on the table, reached into his wallet to leave some money, and walked straight out of the restaurant without a single word." Our eyes are all watering because we're laughing so hard. This is the best story I've ever heard. She's relentless. I almost feel bad for the poor guy.

We finally start to calm down from our fits of laughter, as we're getting stares from the other customers in the restaurant from all of our cackling. I turn to her and rub her back. "That sucks Cass. Sorry you didn't get to have a good evening."

"What do you mean? Of course I had a good

evening. I got to make fun of that idiot for half the night. He paid for a really nice meal. After he left, I got up and sat at the bar. The twenty-eight-year-old hot as sin bartender told me that he overheard our whole conversation, that he thought I was hysterical, and that he would never have 'soft issues' with a woman like me. I ended up going home with him and rocking his world all night long."

She throws her hair back, sips her martini, and finishes with "all's well that ends well, ladies."

My girls and I stare at her. Just when I think Cassandra can't possibly shock us anymore, she does. I shouldn't be surprised. She's been doing it for thirty years.

Reagan holds up her glass of wine in toast. "To Aunt Cass, my idol." We all smile. "You have filled these Sunday night   dinners with endless laughter for the past three years."   Cassandra winks at her.

"To Aunt Cass," we all say.

"Thank you. I try to keep you all entertained." She takes   another sip of her drink. "By the way, I won't be here next   Sunday. I have to leave that afternoon for a week of meetings in San Francisco."

The girls all frown at that. I jump in a bit reluctantly. "Actually girls, Jackson has invited the four of us to a barbecue at his house next Sunday. His three sons will be there as well. Are you guys up for that?"

Skylar responds first. "Wow, Mom. Are you guys that serious already? Having all of your children meet seems pretty serious."

"You should have seen them on the dancefloor on Friday night. Seemed serious to me. It was like watching live porn."

I give her a nasty look. "Thanks, Cass." I turn back to the girls. "It was not porn. We kissed on the dancefloor. I told you, he's very affectionate and seemingly unbothered by a little PDA. It's harmless."

"Harmless? I almost got pregnant just watching you guys."

"Cassandra! Enough! Why don't you leave for San Francisco tonight?" She blows me a kiss. The girls are all giggling.

I turn back to them. "You guys don't have to come. I can tell him you're not ready for it yet."

"Mom, we saw him naked in bed with you holding onto your boobs like a toddler holds their blankie. It's fine. We're happy to go over there. I met him. He couldn't have been nicer. I'm sure his sons are too."

"Thanks, Harley. I actually met one of them on Saturday morning. He seemed very nice."

"Tell them how you met him."

"Cassandra, you're really cruising for it. I'm not telling you anything ever again."

"Oh please. You love it. They're not babies anymore, Dare. Just be happy that I didn't tell them what you did in the limo the night before." I kick her under the table.

Reagan is laughing. "Ooh. Tell us everything."

"No. Only that I met one of his sons in a similar fashion to how Harley met Jackson."

"Sleeping with his hands on your boobs?"

"Not exactly like how Harley met Jackson, but close enough."

"Jesus, Dare. Just tell them. Your Mom woke up naked on top of Jackson. She didn't. realize his son was in the room and she started to go down on him. Jackson put a stop to it before it got too far, but the damage was done." The girls explode with laughter. My face must be beet red.

"Cass, you are officially forever disinvited to our family   dinners."

"Pft. Never. It would be boring without me. I'm the   entertainment." This is true. She is the entertainment.

"We're good Mom. It will be fun. I always wanted brothers," Reagan adds.

"There will be no brothers. Just a nice dinner." They all just smirk at me.

Jackson

It's Monday morning. I had the best weekend with Darian. I can't stop thinking about her. She's just so amazing. Payton is at Abelson's office finalizing the paperwork. I guess I'm on my own for lunch today. I've come to enjoy my daily lunches with Payton. It's nearly noon when Donna buzzes into my office. "Mr. Knight, there's a *very attractive* Darian Lawrence here see you." Darian's here? In my office?

"Thanks, Donna. I'll be right out." I walk out into the   reception area, and sure enough, my beautiful girl is there.

She's in a long, nice, buttoned-up jacket that goes past her knees with sky-high stiletto heels. She must be in court today, or perhaps meeting with a client. She looks gorgeous. Donna has the biggest grin on her face that I've ever seen from her. I immediately go to kiss Darian on the cheek. "What a pleasant surprise. What are you doing here?"

She smiles. "I was in the neighborhood and thought I'd bring you some lunch." She holds up a bag that looks like it has a few boxes in it.

"Wonderful. Thank you. Perfect timing. I'm happy you came by." I rub her cheek with my thumb and stare at her for a   moment too long. I can't help myself.

"Ahem, ahem." Donna interrupts.

"Excuse me. I'm so sorry. Darian Lawrence, please meet Donna Reddick. Donna, this is Darian."

"So nice to meet you, Darian." They shake hands. "You're very pretty, dear."

"Thank you, Donna. It's nice to meet you as well."

"How do you know Mr. Knight?" Donna can't help herself.

"We're, um..."

"Enough with the questions, Donna. Darian is my friend. That's all you need to know. Why don't you leave and go to lunch early. I clearly won't be leaving the office for lunch today, so you can head out now. Please ask one of the associates to man the phone while you're gone."

"Very well. It's lovely to meet you, Darian."

Donna throws her purse strap over her shoulder, looking happy as can be.

"You as well Donna."

Donna grabs her jacket and heads out the door. I show Darian towards my office. As we're walking, I ask, "are you meeting with a client or something? You look beautiful."

She has a bit of a devious smile. "There's someone who has misbehaved and they need to be punished."

As we're walking through my office door, I respond "who?"

She closes the door behind us, locks it, and whispers "me," as she rips off her coat revealing herself in nothing but a red bustier and red lace underwear. Holy shit. I've never seen anything so hot in my entire life.

Her perfect legs look a mile long in those stilettos. Her tits are practically spilling out of the top of her bustier. Her waist is tiny. She's perfection personified. She throws her jacket on a chair and launches herself at me. She flings her arms around my neck and kisses me. I immediately lift her legs and wrap them around my waist, as her tongue licks the seam of my lips begging entry into my mouth. I open for her.

We're kissing long and hard. I fall back into my desk chair with her still on top of me grinding into my now painfully hard dick. She moves off my lips, and kisses and bites down my neck. She whispers, "Mr. Knight, I've been a very naughty secretary. You need to punish me."

I deepen my voice. "What kind of punishment do you want?"

"Well, sir, I guess you get to decide. You're the boss." My dick gets even harder, if possible.

I respond in an even deeper, more authoritative voice. "Well, I don't have a lot of time. It will have to be hard and fast."

"That's just how I like it, sir. I have to get back to your front desk after all." She bats her eyelashes.

In my regular voice, I break character and ask "any rules?"

She bites my lower lip, not too hard, but not that soft. She pulls my lip out as far as it will go until she lets go and it snaps back into place. She whispers into my mouth, "no rules. Whatever you want. Do your worst, sir." I completely snap. I stand up still holding her. I sweep my arm across my desk knocking everything off of it.

I pull her off me and lay her down on the desk on her back. I pull her bustier down exposing her perfect tits. I grab them while pinching and sucking her nipples hard. She arches her back beneath me. She wraps her legs around me begging for some relief. I bite her nipple and tell her, "that pussy will get attention when I'm good and ready. Do you understand me?"

She smiles at my willingness to play the game. She unwraps her legs and says "yes, sir."

I spend a few more minutes biting and sucking her nipples. They're red and hard now. I lift up and slowly rub my finger down the middle of her body and over the outside of her underwear by her pussy. "Do you want me here?" I rub her.

She moans and nods her head. "Yes, sir."

I continue to move my finger along the seam of her   underwear until I reach the area of her back entrance. "What about here?" I look at her in challenge.

She lifts her eyebrow, challenging me right back. "If that's what you want, sir. I'm yours to punish as you please." I almost blow my load from that answer.

I flip her over so her chest is pressed against the desk. She's bent over my desk with her feet on the ground in front of me. I rip her underwear off and run my finger through her pussy. Drenched, per normal. I need to taste it. I get down on my knees and slowly lick her from the front all the way around to the back, giving her back entrance a few extra licks. She moans out in pleasure.

I repeat the trail over and over a few more times. She's dripping wet now. I stand up, rub her ass and spank her. I think it initially shocks her, but after a few seconds, she wiggles are ass begging for more. "You are a bad secretary and must be punished." I spank her again and she moans.

I can physically see her wetness now seeping onto her thighs. I unbuckle my belt, unzip my fly and pull out my severely engorged cock. I run it through her wet lips and smack her pussy with it. "Oh... God...," she moans loudly. I stick two fingers into her to confirm that she's ready for me. She most definitely is.

"Hold on tight." She reaches up and grabs the front of my desk. I pull my fingers out of her, grab her hips and slam into her entrance. She screams out.

I reach around and grab her breasts as my leverage and start to let her have it. Over and over I pound into her. She's trying to contain her screams since we're in my office, but she's not overly successful at it.

Darian is a full-fledged screamer. Her screams only add to my gratification. This is so hot, and I'm definitely not going to last long, but I can already feel a quiver in her walls and know it won't take much more to push her over the edge.

I do want it to last a little longer, so I ease up on my pace, moving in and out of her more slowly now. Long, deep strokes.

I circle my thumb around her back entrance. She turns her head back towards me, lifts the corner of her lips, and looks at me in the eyes. "Jackson, if you do that I'll come right away."

That's the only invitation I need. I increase the pace of my thrusts and then thrust my thumb into her back entrance. She screams in ecstasy while writhing on my desk.

I start moving my thumb at the same pace as my cock. She wasn't kidding. I feel her pussy immediately pulsate and tighten around my cock. I reach around with my other hand and cover her mouth just as she screams into her orgasm, easily pushing me into mine.

I continue pumping until I'm sure she's finished. I pull my thumb and my cock out. I tuck myself back into my pants and zip up.

I bend down and softly kiss her red butt cheek,

gently   rubbing it to soothe it. I pull her up and turn her around. I grab her face and kiss her with everything I have,   appreciating her fulfilling my fantasy here today. She kisses me back the same.

As I pull away, I say, "that's the best lunch I've ever had." She giggles. "Why don't you wash up in the bathroom. I'll clean up my desk and set out our lunch."

"Okay. I'll be right back." She walks over to my private   bathroom and closes the door. I put everything back on my desk, sans an item or two that broke when I swept it off the desk. Totally worth it.

I set up the sandwiches she brought on my conference table, and grab a few waters. She comes out of the bathroom just as I finish. She picks up her torn underwear from the floor and throws it at me. "I'm keeping a tab, Knight. We're up to two pairs."

I smile. "I'm good for it. Come sit." She throws on her jacket and sits at my conference table. We start in on our   sandwiches.

"Another fantasy checked off your list, Knight." She throws a wink my way.

"Darian, you're my walking and talking fantasy, sugar. All this other stuff is just gravy."

"Maybe so, but we're going to have to hit my list soon."

"Got something in mind?"

"I'm working on a little something. I'll let you know when I'm ready."

"Whatever you want. I'm in."

We laugh and talk as we eat our lunch. She tells me she can't see me tonight because she's watching Monday Night   Football with Scott's friends. I'm a little jealous, but I try not to let on. I know it's important to her to maintain that connection. I just don't love the idea of her hanging with a bunch of divorced guys, but I know she doesn't see them that way. She's a guy's girl. It's one of the things I adore about her. I guess she'll always need her time watching sports with the guys. They're just longtime friends. I hope.

CHAPTER 13

Darian

I'm throwing on my jeans and Washington jersey when my doorbell rings. What the hell? I'm not expecting anyone. I've got to leave in the next fifteen minutes if I'm going to get to Alan's house by kickoff. I open the front door but no one is there. I look down and see a box. I open it up. It's ten pairs of lace thongs, in just about every color, with a note.

> *To The Naughtiest Secretary I Know,*
> *To replace those I've ruined and those I plan to ruin in the future. I look forward to punishing you again.*
>
> *Happily,*
> *Your Satisfied Boss*

I smile. He's adorable. I grab my cell to text him.

> *Me: Well played, Knight.*

> *Jackson: I can't wait to see you in them, and then rip them*

off of you.

I shake my head and go to put my cell away when it pings with another text.

Jackson: Don't wear them tonight.

Ouch. I could tell in his office that he wasn't entirely thrilled about my plans for this evening, but this text is definitely pretty clear in that regard. Spending time with Scott's friends is important to me.

If Jackson wants to spend time with me, he's simply going to have to accept it. I should probably tell the boys about Jackson. I don't know how they'll take it. They all see me as Scott's wife.

I arrive at Alan's house about three minutes before kickoff. I see Drew, Nelson, and Paul's cars already in the driveway. They all graduated high school with Scott. It's a weird thing about people from Philadelphia. They never live more than a few miles from where they grew up. Growing up in Washington DC, which by nature is a more transient town, people just aren't like that. My high school friends live all over the country. One even lives overseas. What can I say? People from Philadelphia are like a cult. They all get mad when I say that, but it's true.

Alan hugs me hello. "You're cutting it close,

Dare."

"Sorry, I'm here. I got tied up. Where's my beer?" Alan hands me my favorite beer, while Paul and Drew hug me hello as well. "Where's Nelson? I saw his car. I know he's here."

Drew laughs. "The she-devil called." That's our name for his ex-wife. We never call her by her actual name anymore. "He's in the other room dealing with more of her bullshit."

Poor Nelson. He got divorced seven years ago and he's still   dealing with nonsense from her. I feel bad for their kids. They're the real victims of this. I never really got along with her. She used to accuse me of having a thing for Nelson, and Nelson for me. She would lose her shit every time I spoke to him. She's insane. I've never had anything but brotherly   affection for Nelson, and I know he feels similarly towards me.

Up until I met Jackson a few weeks ago, I can honestly say I've never had any remote feelings for another man besides my husband since the day he asked me out. Scott always said that she is just jealous because men find me attractive and they don't find her attractive, but I don't know. It always bothered me. It's kind of insulting to be accused of that.

Yes, I'm a guy's girl and always have been. I've always had guys as friends. But, while I hang with guys, I'm not a flirt by any stretch of the imagination. Things were always weird with her. I wasn't exactly devastated or surprised when they announced that they were separating, and eventually divorcing.

The game starts and we're all cheering except for Nelson, who is still missing. At some point during the first quarter, he comes back into the living room. "Sorry guys. The she-devil is at it again." We all look at him with sympathy. "Hey, Dare. I didn't see you before. Good to see you, gorgeous."

I give him a hug. "Hey, Nelson. Good to see you too. Sorry you're dealing with this shit."

"Me too."

We do our normal thing for the first half. Cheering, playing a few drinking games, talking fantasy football smack. They've all resigned themselves to the fact that I win our fantasy football league every year. Halftime approaches, and I know this is our only time for any real talk.

"Hey guys. Can I talk to you for a minute?"

Alan looks at me. "Of course, Dare. Is everything okay with you and the girls?"

"Yes, we're fine. Honestly, for the first time in three years, I'm starting to *actually* feel fine. Um... I... um... well, I sort of started seeing someone." You could hear a pin drop for what feels like an eternity as four stunned faces stare at me. They must be upset thinking that I've moved on from Scott. I start to feel the need to speak, since no one else is. "I mean, it hasn't been that long, and we haven't fully defined our relationship, but we're definitely together. He's a really nice guy." I'm rambling in an attempt to avoid silence.

Drew stands up and comes over to hug me. He gives me a smile that doesn't quite reach his eyes. "Dare, I think that's great. I really do. You know we all want to see you happy. Are you happy?"

I nod. "It's the closest I've been to happy in three years."

"Well then, fantastic. I'm happy for you."

Paul grabs my hand. "Dare, you're obviously a stunning woman. It was only a matter of time before you started dating. I'm sure there are men lining up at your door. Is it a little weird for us to think of you with someone that isn't Scott? Of course. You were Darian and Scott for twenty-five years. But Scott isn't here and you deserve to live your life. You really haven't been doing that."

"I know I haven't. My kids and my friends have been telling me that for a long time. But I needed to do things on my schedule. The time was finally right for me."

Alan smiles. "Do we know the lucky guy?"

"I don't think so. I guess he's sort of Philebrity, but I doubt you'd know him."

"Is a Philebrity supposed to be the Philadelphia version of a celebrity," Alan asks laughing. "That's hysterical. I've never heard that term."

I laugh with him. Hopefully, this breaks the tension because it's palpable. "Yes, it's someone who's Philadelphia famous but not real world famous."

"What's his name?"

"Jackson Knight."

Alan pinches his eyebrows together as if trying to remember something. He gets up and goes into the bathroom. He returns with a stack of magazines. He flips through them until he gets to the one he wants.

He shows me the cover of 'Philly Life' from a few years ago, and sure enough, Jackson is on the front. It's the hottest bachelors over forty issue. "Is this him?" I nod. They all gather around and read the article. I already read it online a few weeks ago when Jackson and I were just talking on the phone. I know what it says.

Drew looks up first, wide-eyed. "So it sounds like this guy could get any woman he wanted."

Nelson looks at Drew. "What is that supposed to mean, Drew? If I could date any woman I wanted, I would choose Dare." That's kind of a weird comment. They're all staring at Nelson. There's something unspoken going on among all of them right now.

Drew jumps in. "What I meant, Nelson, was that she needs to be careful with a guy like this. He's probably a player."

This just got uncomfortable really fast. I need to do something. I grab the magazine. "Guys, relax. I know about this. He hates it. He thinks it's a joke. It's not a big deal. Jackson is a humble guy. He's definitely not a player. I promise. He's been nothing but good to me."

Alan kisses my head. "Okay, sweetie. If you say so. We're all just looking out for you."

"I appreciate it. Don't worry about it. Like I said, it's fairly new. I'm just happy to be getting out there." I motion my head   towards the television. "The second half is about to start. Let's forget this and get back to the game. Does everyone need another beer?" They all nod. I jump up and grab another round for everyone. I need a moment away from their stares.

Much of the second half is watched in silence. There's   definitely an elephant in the room now. It's awkward as hell. Paul, Drew and Nelson leave right when the game is over, each giving me a warm goodbye. I stick around for a few minutes to help Alan clean up. I thank him and hug him goodbye. "Dare, are you sure this guy is a good guy? The last thing you need is another broken heart."

I smile at him. "Alan, I know your worry comes from a good place. We're casual. There are no hearts involved. Nothing is getting broken here." I'm not sure this is true, but I know he needs to hear it. "And he's definitely a good guy. That much I know already. I'm having fun. I need some of that in my life."

"Okay, sweetie. Please just be careful."

"I will. Good night, Alan."

"Good night, Dare."

I close his front door and start heading towards my car when I hear a voice. "I didn't know you were ready to start dating." I startle as I see Nelson appear from the shadows. I thought he left like fifteen minutes ago.

"Nelson, you scared me."

"Sorry. So when did you decide you were ready to start dating?"

"It's not like I woke up one morning and said today is the day. Cassandra has been trying to get me to go out for over a year. I finally went one night and I met Jackson."

He rolls his eyes. "I should have known Cassandra was   involved. Where's there's smoke there's fire."

"What is that supposed to mean, Nelson?

"It means she's trouble and I don't want her dragging you down into her debaucherous world. You're too good for that, Dare. You're not a slut who sleeps around like she is."

I'm getting mad. "Don't disrespect my best friend. Who she does and doesn't sleep with is none of your concern. It has no bearing on her as a person. There is no better friend on this planet. No one has been there for me more in the past three years than Cassandra. Is she a little unconventional at times? Yes. But she's been there for me when I've been at my lowest and she loves me. She only wants me to finally start to heal and move on."

"I want that too, Dare. I want you to heal and move on." He stares at me for a moment. "But I want it to be with me." I'm stunned into silence. "If I knew you were ready, I would have asked you out. I've waited for twenty-eight years for you to be available." What?

"When Scott and I were in business school, I was with him that night he saw you in the library.

You were so young, only twenty, and so damn beautiful. I went with him to that library every night for two weeks waiting for you to come back so that asshole could ask you out. The fact that he saw you two   seconds before me is my biggest regret in life. It should have been me."

"Don't disrespect Scott by calling him an asshole. He wasn't an asshole. He was your best friend. You're the asshole right now."

"I'm sorry. I didn't mean it that way." I'm not going to tell him it's okay because it's not.

I can't handle this. "Nelson, I need to go."

"Go out with me."

"No."

"Why?"

"Because I'm seeing someone."

"It won't last. This guy is a player. I can tell. He's no good for you."

I feel the tears welling in my eyes. "He's not a player. Even if he wasn't in the picture, it would still be no."

"Why?"

"I'm sorry, but I don't see you that way. You're Scott's friend and you're an extension of him. He saw you as a brother and so do I. I would never do that to Scott." Nelson goes to grab my arm. I pull my arm away. "Get off me. Don't touch me." The tears are rolling.

I hear Alan yell from the front door. "Get the fuck off of her, Nelson!" He comes out and pushes Nelson away from me. "Get in your car and go home, Nelson. You need to cool off."

"Fine. Whatever. This is bullshit. You're all fucking in love with her. I'm just the only one with the balls to admit it." I'm again stunned into silence. I have no clue what's going on. I don't think I can stand anymore. I feel like the wind has been knocked out of me. I sit on the front steps and start crying. Nelson gets in his car and drives away.

Alan sits down next to me. "I'm sorry that happened, Dare. I'm sorry he said what he did. I'm sorry he touched you. He knows better."

"Alan, I don't even know what just happened."

"Dare, Nelson has been in love with you for twenty-eight years. We all knew it. The she-devil knew it. Sweetie, Scott knew it. Scott and Nelson fought about it many times over the years. You had no idea?"

I shake my head no. "Scott never told me. I... I didn't realize any of this."

"No, why would he. I get it. Scott wasn't as

insecure after you guys got married, but those first two years when you were dating, Scott was terrified that Nelson would steal you away. They came to blows at least a dozen times in those two years. There's a reason you've never been allowed to be alone with Nelson. Scott wouldn't allow it. He and Nelson got into so many fights over you throughout the years. More at the beginning, but they'd still happen from time to time when he'd catch Nelson staring at you." What the fuck? How did I miss this?

Tears are free falling from my eyes. I eventually croak out, "what about what he said about the rest of you? Is that true?"

He takes a deep breath. "I don't know, Dare. They don't make many women like you. You're like this completely perfect woman. No woman can hold a candle to you. It's probably why we're all so fucked up in our respective relationships and none of our marriages lasted. None of us could find anyone in your ballpark. Do I think there have been times over the past twenty-eight years that each of us has wished you were ours? If I'm being honest, yes, I do. Any man with eyes and ears would. But Nelson is next level. He's just always had it in his mind that you were meant to be with him and not Scott. I'm sorry you have to deal with this. It shouldn't have happened. I really meant these Monday night gatherings as a way to get you out of the house and have some fun, Dare. Our way of checking in on you to make sure you're doing alright. I promise there was nothing more involved. I was just trying to be a good friend to Scott by having you over each week. I wanted to be a good friend to you as well."

I can see the truth of that statement in his eyes. "I know you were Alan. You're a good guy." We're silent for a few minutes. "I don't think I can come back here again though."

"I know, sweetie. I'm sorry for that. But the good news is that it sounds like you're ready to spread your wings and fly again. I'm happy for you. I really am."

"Maybe." It's time for me to go. I don't think I can even hug him goodbye. I get up, wave, whisper goodbye, and get into my car. I drive away with the tears flowing down my cheeks. I pick up my phone and call the only person who can make me feel good right now.

I dial the number and the phone rings. I hear a sleepy voice. "Hey, sugar. I didn't think I was going to hear from you   tonight. I'm so happy you called. I miss you in my bed." I smile at the mere sound of his voice. It soothes me. His sleepy voice is actually kind of sexy too.

"I'm sorry, were you sleeping?" I tried to get that out without sounding like I'm crying, but I clearly fail.

"Darian, what's wrong? Are you okay?" He sounds more alert.

"Can I come over?"

"Of course you can. Do you want me to come and get you? Where are you?"

"No, I'll be there in a little bit. I'll see you then." I hang up and drive to Jackson's house.

Fifteen minutes later I pull into his driveway. He's standing outside by his door in his boxer briefs and an opened button-down shirt he must have just thrown on. His hair is sticking up all over the place like he's been running his fingers through it.

As soon as I stop, he runs over to my car door barefoot. He opens it. It's clear that I've been crying the whole way over. "Oh my God. Are you hurt?" He starts moving my clothing around looking for an injury.

I grab his hands. "Stop. I'm not physically injured."

He lets out a deep breath as he undoes my seatbelt and helps me from the car. He puts his arms around me and lets me cry in silence into his chest for a few minutes.

I eventually pull back a bit. Just enough so that I can look at his face. He tucks some stray strands of hair behind my ear and wipes the tears from underneath my eyes. I look up at him. Everything about him soothes me. The way he looks. The way he smells, so uniquely Jackson. The way he touches me and holds me with such affection.

"Jackson," I say softly, "I need something from you tonight but if it's too much to ask and you're not up for it, just tell me."

"I'll do anything you want. Anything to make you feel better."

I know he means that too. I rub his 5:00 shadow with my fingertips. He's so gorgeous. I look at him in the eyes. "I need you to make me feel good." I'm silent for a beat. "I need you to make love to me."

Without a moment of hesitation, he nods. Without another word, he closes my car door, scoops me up into his arms like a bride with my arms around his neck, and walks straight into his house.

He closes the door with his foot and walks us to his bedroom. He places me down so I'm sitting on the bed.

With no sense of urgency, he removes my shoes and socks. He takes my hand to help me up. He pulls my jersey up and over my head. He unbuttons and unzips my jeans to pull them off.

He slowly kisses his way back up my legs first, then my body, then my neck, and eventually ending with a soft kiss to my lips. He takes off my bra and tosses it to the side.

He slides the backs of his fingers down the sides of my body until he reaches my underwear. He loops his fingers through the top and pulls them down and off my legs.
He removes his own shirt and boxer briefs. We both stand there completely naked.

He softly runs the back of his hand over my cheek and breaks the silence. "Darian, you're so incredibly beautiful to me."

He pulls the sheets back and helps me to lay down on my back. He lays down on top of me, between my legs, and pulls the sheets and blanket back over us. He continues to run both of his thumbs over my cheeks, staring at me with so much affection.

He slowly moves his lips to mine and takes them in a tender kiss. We kiss and kiss without any hurry to move things along. He runs his fingertips up and down the sides of my body at a leisurely pace, as he kisses me.

I hold his face in my hands and stare at him, conveying my appreciation for how he's handling this moment of need from me. "Make love to me Jackson."

He moves his fingers between my legs to make sure that I'm ready for him. I'm always ready for him. He then moves   himself to my entrance and so very slowly enters my body inch by heavenly inch until he's all the way in.

Given his extreme size, there's really no way to adequately describe the few moments after Jackson enters my body. It's an intense feeling of pleasure simply taking its time spreading throughout my body.

As the pleasure trickles in, everything else going on in my life and in the world trickles out and fades into the background. It's among my favorite few moments of every time we're intimate. And tonight, it's just what I need.

The toxic emotions of tonight fade away, as Jackson and utter bliss are consuming me. He pulls my hands above my head, and interlaces his fingers with mine. He takes my lips in his again, as he starts to move slowly inside my body.

I'm entirely consumed by him right now. He feels so good.

There's no rush as he moves in and out. He is making sure to give me exactly what I need in this moment. I'm grateful to him for taking care of me like this.

He eventually removes one hand from mine

above our heads, and takes both hands in the other, softly holding and caressing them with his fingers. The free hand now gently moves down my arm. He takes my breast and teases my nipple until it's completely hardened. He breaks his mouth from mine and kisses his way down to my breast. He traces slow circles with his tongue around my nipple and eventually takes my nipple into his mouth and sucks. That's the tipping point for me sending me into utter bliss.

My whole body is quivering as I moan Jackson's name. Once he's sure I've ridden out my release, Jackson finds his own.

After he's done, he takes my face in his hands and gives me a slow, lazy, passionate kiss. I have tears welling in my eyes, slightly overcome with the emotion of what's gone on here tonight. I whisper, "thank you, Jackson." He nods in understanding of my tears and kisses me one more time as he slides his weight off of my body, immediately snuggling me into his side.

We lay there with his arm around me and my head on his chest. I'm tracing my fingers along his chest and stomach. He gives me time to digest the events of the evening, but eventually breaks the silence. "Do you want to talk about what upset you tonight?"

I think I owe him that much. "Okay." I swallow hard. I can't look at him. I keep my head on his chest as I speak. "One of Scott's friends came onto me tonight. He told me that he's had feelings for me for twenty-eight years. He told me that I belong with him." I can feel Jackson's arm tense around me.

"What brought this about? Why is he telling you this now?"

"I told them about you. I told them that I was seeing   someone and finally having fun and experiencing a little bit of   happiness in my life. I thought they'd be happy for me. These guys were like brothers to Scott. They've taken care of me like brothers since he died. I thought I owed it to them to tell them about you. I didn't expect the reaction I received."

He's running his finger up and down my arm in comfort. "How did the others take it?"

"It was a little weird at first. They were silent. Awkwardly so. I thought they were just surprised that I was already dating."

"Already? Darian, it's been over three years. The last thing you did was rush into this."

"I know. You're right. But in the moment, that's what I thought. Then they sort of said they just wanted me to be happy, but when they asked your name, and I gave it, one of them recognized it. He had the eligible bachelors magazine in his bathroom, and he brought it out for them all to see."

"I hate that stupid article. Freaking Donna made me do it. I must have been out of my mind to listen to her. I wish I never did it."

"I know it's not really who you are. Then they all got into it with me about you probably being a player. That I need to be careful with you." He squeezes me again. "I assured them that you are not like that and that I'm fine."

"So when did the one guy tell you his feelings?"

"His name is Nelson. He kind of accosted me when I was alone getting into my car to leave for the evening. He told me that he was with Scott when Scott first saw me all those years ago, and that he fell for me too. I learned that he and Scott argued about it for years, even physically fighting. I never knew any of this. It was really hard to take."

"Did he touch you?"

"He grabbed my arm at one point but I was able to pull it away. Another of the guys, Alan, came outside at that point and pushed him away from me. He asked Nelson to leave."

"Did he?"

"Yes. That's when Alan explained that Nelson and Scott often fought about me. I almost feel like there's been this big secret that Scott kept from me. I don't know what to make of it. This came out of leftfield for me."

"I'm sure Scott just didn't want to upset you. He was protecting you. I would have done the same." I smile that Jackson is   defending Scott. Even Scott's own best friend couldn't manage that.

"Before Nelson left, he mentioned that all the guys have had some feelings for me. Alan sort of confirmed it later on." I take a deep breath. "These were Scott's lifetime best friends. I just don't understand it."

"Darian, do you see yourself? I mean really see yourself? You have an inner and outer beauty that simply radiates. There's not a man alive that wouldn't want to be with you. I have no doubt that the men who have been in your life for decades pine after you."

I kiss his chest. "I don't know what to say. I never saw it."

"That doesn't surprise me in the least. Humility is one of those inner traits. It wouldn't even occur to you."

"It doesn't matter. I don't see them that way. I never have. I never will." I swallow hard to get my next sentence out. "The only man that I'm interested in right now is you."

He kisses the top of my head and rubs my body. "Good, because I'm not letting you go without a fight."

"There's no need for fighting."

"Are you going to see them again? I know you're accustomed to seeing them weekly."

"I don't think I can." I feel him let out the breath he was clearly holding. "At least not for a while until things cool off. I truly only see these guys as surrogate brothers. I think I'm still in shock." I kiss his chest again and look up at him. "Thank you for giving me what I needed tonight. I can't tell you how much I appreciate it. It was perfect. You're perfect."

"Making love to you is the most natural thing I do. You never need to thank me for it." I don't really want to dig deeper into that comment right now, so I let the conversation end there. We eventually fall asleep in the comfort of one another's arms.

The next day is my lunch with Skylar. I arrive a few minutes early to get a table, and order us both a glass of wine. We're going to need it. Skylar arrives right on time. She looks adorable in a short flowy skirt, t-shirt and denim jacket. She has long, skinny legs. She's probably got three inches on me. She has blonde wavy hair with big green eyes. She's blossomed into a stunning young woman.

I get up to hug and kiss her hello. "Hey, baby doll. You look pretty."

"Thanks Mom. So do you."

"How's school going?"

"It's fine. It's my last year, so the classes are small. No more big lectures. I prefer it that way. I know all of the professors in the business department at this point." School has always come easily to Skylar.

"How is the GMAT studying coming along? I'm happy to hire you a tutor to help."

"No, it's fine. I'm scoring high on my practice tests. The exam is in a few weeks. I think I'll do well. If I don't, I'll still have time to get a tutor and take the test again. I do need to start filling out my business school applications though."

"I'm happy to help with those if you want. Have you narrowed down your list of schools?"

"I think I'd like to stay here. I don't want to leave you alone."

I smile. "Baby, I'm not alone. You don't need to stay here if you don't want to. There are a lot of good schools out there that would be lucky to have you." She scrunches her nose. "Why don't you at least apply to a wide variety of schools and then make your decision in the spring. It's better to have options."

"Yea, I guess that makes sense."

"You know, I have your sisters. They're not going anywhere anytime soon. And I couldn't get rid of Aunt Cass if I tried, so I'm stuck with her." We both smile at that.

"What about this Jackson guy? You must be getting pretty serious if you're having all of your children meet one another."

"Jackson is wonderful. I'm enjoying my time with him, but it's very new. We'll see. You kids have a lot in common. Jackson thought it would be nice to meet, and put some faces to names. Obviously, I brag about my girls all the time." She smiles. "Anyway, I didn't come down here to talk about my guy. I came to talk about yours." She rolls her eyes. "What's the story, Skylar? You don't seem too happy with him."

"Did Harley and Reagan put you up to this? Those bitches won't leave me alone about him. They don't like him but they have no real reason to feel that way. He's never been anything but nice to them when they come out with us."

"I think they're just concerned that he's messing with your head. So am I. You said he keeps disappearing on you. Do you have any clue what's going on?"

"I don't, and I'll talk to him soon, but I don't think it's what they think it is. They think he's seeing another girl. It's not that."

"What makes you so sure?"

"Honestly, I've been there the last few times he's reappeared. He smells and looks like shit. I think he has some sort of night job he's not proud of. We don't talk about money, but I don't think he comes from any. I'm pretty sure he pays his own way here. I'm honestly starting to think he may just have some really crappy job that he's embarrassed to tell me about."

"If that's the case, then that's certainly very noble. Regardless, you deserve to know what's going on. You need to talk to him."

She stirs her drink with her straw. "Yea, I guess. I don't want to embarrass him though. I don't care if he has money or not. I don't care if he has some shitty job. He's good to me when we're together."

"Of course you don't care about the money or him having a crappy job. It's about keeping secrets. It's never healthy for any relationship." My mind goes to having learned last night that Scott kept a secret from me. I shake it.

"I got it. I like him. I have fun with him. Can we move on?" I nod. "Let's interrogate you about Jackson. Tell me about his children."

"I've only met one. Trevor. He's twenty-three years old and in business school. He's very cute and has a good personality. He looks exactly like Jackson, just the slightly younger version. Kind of like Harley and I. Trevor has a fraternal twin, Hayden. He's in medical school here. His oldest son is Payton. He's 30 years old, married, and works with Jackson. I think they're all pretty close."

"What's the story with the ex-wife?"

"I don't know much other than it's been about five years since they divorced, it seems to be very amicable, and they had to get married young because she became pregnant with Payton when they were sophomores in college. He's confessed to me that they were never really in love. Just doing what they had to do for the sake of their kids."

"Oh jeez. That sucks. I can't imagine having a baby that young."

"Not ideal. That's for sure. But he managed to get educated and build a very successful business. He's quite impressive. He's actually philanthropic too, which I love about him."

"Mom, you're in looooooooove."

"No, I'm not. Cut it out."

"Sunday is going to be fun." I roll my eyes.

CHAPTER 14

Darian

"Hey, baby. It's been kind of a weird week. I'm a little upset with you for not telling me about Nelson's feelings for me. It all came to a head on Monday night and it's not great. I don't think Alan, Drew and Paul are even talking to Nelson right now. I'm not sure I'm talking to any of them. It's all a bit messed up. I wish you told me what was going on. I would have been better prepared for it. I feel like I can't spend time with those guys anymore, and it kills me. They were a part of you that I got to hang onto, and now I feel like it's gone."

I pause as I look around for any signs. Nothing. "How ironic is it that all those years I thought the she-devil was crazy about being jealous of me when it came to Nelson's attention, and it turns out she was right." I almost laugh at that. I spent so many years not understanding her, thinking she was insane. She may have been the most sane one of all of us.

"Anyway, I'm still seeing Jackson. He actually helped me a lot when the boys went a little crazy on Monday night. I think you'd like Jackson. He's a good man like you. He treats me really well."

"The girls are all thriving. Reagan actually has a big meeting tomorrow night about franchising. It's just the early stages of planning, but she's really excited about it. I'll let you know how it goes. Skylar is getting ready to apply to business school. I think she feels obligated to stay close to me. I can't tell if she's using me as an excuse to stay close to home, or if she really wants to leave but is afraid of leaving me. I told her that I don't feel so alone anymore. I know Harley and Reagan will be close by for a long time. Cass is, well, Cass. And now I have Jackson." I hesitate for a moment.

"I wanted to let you know that the girls are meeting   Jackson and his sons this Sunday night. Harley met Jackson once before, but Reagan and Skylar haven't. I'm excited for them all to meet. What do you think?" I look around. Nothing.

"Okay. One day you'll let me know your thoughts. Bye baby. I love you always. I'll see you next Friday."

Harley

We're on our way to Jackson's house to meet his family, and for my sisters to meet Jackson. While we're certainly happy for Mom, this whole thing is a little freaky for us. We pull up to the house. It's huge and modern, on a tremendous lot. This guydefinitely has some real money. At least we don't have to worry about him being with Mom for her money.

When the car pulls to a stop, she turns to us. "Thank you girls for coming tonight. I know it's a little awkward. If at any point it becomes too much, and you want to leave, of course we can. I'm sure it will be hard to see me with someone that's not your father. I totally understand. I struggle with it at times too. You guys know that I loved your father with all of my heart." That's actually the first time she's ever referred to her love for him in the past tense. I don't think she realized that she did it.

"You know it's taken me a long time to even think about   dating. I'm not sure I thought I was ready until Jackson came into my life. Just know that he's so special and so good to me, but you girls are the most important people in the world to me. I love you so much. I'm just hoping that you're willing to get to know him."

Skylar is sobbing. "For Christ sake Mom. Don't make us cry right before we walk in. Of course we're okay with it." Reagan and I nod in agreement.

"I'm not saying this isn't a little weird, but if Jackson makes you happy, and is going to be in your life, of course we want to get to know him. I can't promise we won't have our emotional moments in seeing you with someone that isn't Dad, but that doesn't mean we're not okay with this. We are." That's the truth. The three of us have discussed it a lot. Mom literally didn't leave the house for three years. She didn't smile. She didn't laugh. She was a shell of the Mom we knew growing up. I wasn't sure we'd ever get her back. We want her to be happy and have someone, as long as it's the right someone.

Now I'm tearing up. "Mom, obviously there's been a huge change in you this past month. You've come back to life. If he's responsible for that, we like him already." Now Mom starts to tear up too.

Reagan, never one to let things stay heavy, adds, "Mom, we're just happy you're finally getting laid. You really needed it. That's probably why you're smiling again." We all start   laughing.

I hear Mom mumble "truth" under her breath as she gets out of the car. There seems to be no topic off-limits in our family. I wouldn't have it any other way. The four of us get out of the car and walk towards the front door. Mom made a salad. I have some wine that I brought, while Reagan and Skylar each made a dessert. Mom has made sure we all know to never go to someone's house empty-handed.

We ring the doorbell. An extremely attractive man in his   twenties, who actually looks a lot like a younger Jackson, opens the door. He has a big smile on his face as he looks us all up and down. He yells back into the house, "Dad! Did you order us models? You're legit the best Dad ever. I love you." He winks at us. "Come in ladies."

Mom playfully slaps his chest and gives him a hug. "Flattery will get you everywhere, Trevor." Trevor smiles down at her and then at each of us as we walk in.

He mumbles, "I mean, I wasn't totally kidding." He holds his hands up in invitation for us to come further into the house and starts singing, "here's the story, of a lovely lady, who was bringing up three very lovely girls. All of them had hair of gold, like their mother, the youngest one in curls. Here's the story, of a man named Knight, who was busy with three boys of his own. They were four men, living all together, yet they were all alone." My sisters and I start cracking up. I like this guy.

Jackson comes to the foyer area and throws Trevor in a   headlock to cut him off. "Please ignore him, ladies. He hasn't quite evolved yet." We all laugh.

Reagan speaks first. "I'm now thinking that a Brady Bunch-themed Christmas card might be appropriate this year. Think of the possibilities." We laugh again. This time Trevor joins.

Jackson gives Mom a quick peck on the lips in greeting, along with a long hug. Reagan mouths to me, "he's hot." I don't even know if she's talking about Jackson or Trevor. They're both hot. They look exactly alike.

Two more insanely attractive men come over, though they don't look anything like Jackson and Trevor. Reagan mouths "they're all hot. What the fuck?"

Jackson then warmly hugs me hello. "Good to see you again, Harley."

He turns to my sisters. "You must be Reagan and Skylar. It's great to meet you both. I've heard so much about you." He offers both of my sisters hugs too. This guy is definitely   affectionate.

"Harley, Reagan, Skylar, please meet my boys Payton and Hayden. I see you already had the unfortunate experience of meeting Trevor." We all shake hands hello. Hayden looks very nervous.

Jackson puts his arm around Mom and pulls her close.   "Payton and Hayden, this is my Darian." My Darian. Mom breaks his hold and hugs both Payton and Hayden hello. Apparently, we're one big hugging family now.

Mom looks around into the house. "Payton, is Kylie here? I was hoping to meet her."

"Unfortunately not. She's been on a cruise with her   girlfriends." Ugh cruises. Gross. Our family hates cruises. "She actually gets back late tonight. I can't wait to see her. I've missed her." Aw. This guy is sweet. I need to find me one of these. I seem to only attract assholes.

Mom smiles warmly at him. "You may not look as much like your father, but you're certainly sweet like him. I'm sorry to have missed her. Maybe next time. Congratulations on your recent wedding."

"Thank you."

Jackson motions for us all to follow him into the house. It's gorgeous, and we only really see the main living area and   kitchen. I can't imagine what the rest looks like. We head straight to the backyard area which has an amazing setup with a pool, outdoor kitchen area, grill and firepit. The fire is lit and whatever he's cooking smells amazing. There's a big seating area set up with appetizers and a bar. Jackson motions for us all to sit and turns to Hayden.

"Hayden, why don't you take everyone's drink orders. I have Darian taken care of." He hands mom her drink of choice, Tito's with club soda and a boatload of limes. This guy is good.

He sits next to her and pulls her close to him with his arm around her. Yep, this is weird to see. Mom with a man that isn't Dad. She mentioned that Jackson is affectionate, but hearing it and seeing it are two different things. Skylar stares at me, clearly thinking the same thing.

Hayden takes our drink orders, and Reagan being Reagan goes right for the jugular. "So, which one of you has seen my mom's boobs? I mean besides Jackson."

Trevor doubles over with laughter. "Oh my God. I love my new sisters. It was me. I had that distinct pleasure." He turns to Mom and winks. "And it *was* a pleasure, Darian."

Mom turns eight shades of red. Jackson playfully smacks the back of his head. "Cut it out. Show some respect."

"Sorry, *Mom*." He laughs again. Trevor is a handful.

Reagan is equal to the task though. "Did you guys know that Harley walked in on your Dad and our Mom too? Harley was kind enough to put us on FaceTime first though, so we all got to enjoy it. I have screenshots if you want to see them."

She starts to take out her phone but Mom

grabs it. "Reagan, enough. Delete those. Jackson, perhaps Trevor and Reagan are the twins here. Maybe there was a mix-up at the hospital."

"They certainly are two peas in a pod," he agrees with a smirk.

Hayden returns with our drinks. His hands are literally   shaking when he gives me mine. "I'm sorry. I'm a little   nervous."

"Oh, it's no problem. Let me help." I grab my drink from him.

Trevor looks over. "Oh my God, Hayden. Just ask her for her autograph, maybe grab a selfie and call it a day." Huh? "Let's get this all out. Harley, Hayden is low-key obsessed with you. Apparently, you're sort of a legend at the medical school." What? I am? For what? Shit. That can't be good.

Hayden stares daggers at Trevor. "Trevor, you suck. Sorry Dr. Lawrence. My brother is a jerk."

"Hayden, I'm like five minutes older than you. Call me Harley." I look at Mom in bewilderment, and she mouths "I'll tell you later."

Everyone kind of goes around in a circle and says a little bit about themselves. Payton is quite impressive. He's a smart guy. It's actually really nice that he loves working with his Dad so much. Jackson grabs my Mom's hand. "Darian, come inside with me to grab the steaks. We need to get them going on the grill." He pulls her in pretty aggressively. What is that about?

I chat with Hayden about medical school. He's struggling a bit with the memorization. I give him a few tips of the trade and he seems grateful. I hear Payton and Reagan talking about her franchising meeting. He gives her some negotiation tips.   Skylar and Payton talk about business school. I can't really hear, but she mentions possibly looking at schools away from home. This is the first I'm hearing of that.

Mom and Jackson return about twenty minutes later. They've clearly been going at it. Both of their lips are red and puffy. Her lipstick is gone and her hair is a mess. They're kind of cute. The six of us all knowingly stare at one another and smirk.

Jackson cooks the steaks and Mom helps to serve the sides. We eventually sit down at the table. I look at Jackson. "This all looks great. Thank you."

"My pleasure. It's nice to have so many beautiful ladies at our table."

Trevor adds, "I'll say. Darian, you're a lawyer, right?"

"I am. Are you in trouble? That would not shock me in the least," she jokes with him and he smiles.

"I am not. Yet. Asking for a friend here, but what are the laws on step-siblings dating?" Everyone laughs.

Hayden shakes his head. "Sorry ladies, but my brother didn't mature past the age of seven."

That's kind of how the meal goes. Lots of poking fun and laughs. Just getting to know one another. It's actually kind of nice. We didn't grow up with brothers. They're pretty relentless with one another, though we do have Reagan in the regard. When the meal is over I suggest that since Mom and Jackson did the heavy lifting on the front end, the six of us clean up, letting Mom and Jackson start on the s'mores by the firepit. Everyone agrees.

The six of us bring everything inside and have an assembly line going, though we all stop when we see Mom and Jackson interact outside. She's sitting on his lap. They're feeding each other s'mores while laughing and kissing. Payton is the first to speak. He nods his head in the direction of Mom and Jackson. "What do you guys make of this?"

Reagan responds. "She's really into him. I don't know how much you guys know about us, but I assume you know our Dad died three years ago. Mom has been miserable since. At least until she started seeing your Dad. She literally barely left the house for three years until they started dating."

Payton responds. "We knew she was a widow, but we didn't know the other stuff. He's like a different man since they started dating. He's more relaxed and amenable at the office. He's not working all hours. He can't wait to get out of the office to see her. I literally heard him whistling in his office the other day. I've never once heard my Dad whistle in thirty years."

He pauses for a moment and changes his expression to a more contemplative one. "Not to be a jerk, but I don't want to see him hurt. While I'm thrilled for him, frankly I'm worried about him if this doesn't work out. I think he's fallen hard and fast. Is she even ready for a relationship?"

It's a fair point. "There are no guarantees. If you're asking me as her daughter, I think she's ready. I like that it happened very naturally. Just two people who met and were attracted to one another. Kind of old school. No fix-up, no dating apps, nothing contrived. They also spent a lot of hours on the phone getting to know one another before their first real date. I think they've done it the right way." I look at them outside laughing. "They're kind of cute together."

Hayden asks, "is it weird to see your mother with a different guy than your father? Did your parents get along?"

"Yes", I answer right away. "They got along *really* well. They had a good marriage. That's why his death was so hard on her. I can't speak for my sisters, but I'd say it's weird to see her with someone else, but not bad weird. Just different weird. We don't want her miserable. He seems to make her happy. That's what we want. He's literally the most affectionate man I've ever seen. They can't keep their hands off of one another. Did you notice that he's always touching her? Even when they were eating his hands were on her leg. I assume you all saw what they looked like when they came back outside earlier. Look at them now."

Everyone else looks outside. They're practically licking the marshmallows off of each other.

"This is really strange for us", Trevor adds. "Dad was not like this with our mother. They were never affectionate with each other. I don't ever even remember them kissing. I don't think they were really in love. We've never seen him like this. He's totally smitten."

"I think we should all be happy that our parents are happy. My mother is the fucking best. She deserves this. Watching her these past three years was painful. She barely made it out the door to my college graduation two years ago, and now she's literally sucking a marshmallow off of a hot guy's lips looking like she's two seconds away from tearing his clothes off. I'm all in for this." Reagan is most definitely a big supporter of this relationship.

Trevor gives her the evil eye. "Please don't ever call our Dad a 'hot guy' again."

She stares right back at him. "You're his mini-me, you should be happy."

"There's nothing mini about me, sweetheart." He winks at Reagan and she rolls her eyes.

Hayden jumps in. "So I think we all agree it's a good thing?" We all nod yes. I look up at Payton and he eventually reluctantly nods. The evening ends with us all enjoying the s'mores by the fire. Everyone needs to be up early the next morning, so we all say our goodbyes.

Mom is driving me home before she returns to Jackson's for the evening. Trevor and Hayden live near Reagan and Skylar, so they offered to drive them home. She asks, "did you have an okay time, sweetie?"

"I did. They're all really nice. Even Trevor." She smiles. "Looks like you had a good time. You certainly made sure that Jackson was clean of marshmallows."

She bites her lip and scrunches up her face. "You could see that?"

"We were *all* watching you guys. You're adorable. The boys said that Jackson wasn't like that in his marriage."

"Yes, he's mentioned it wasn't a very loving marriage."

"Does that worry you?"

"No. They were very young and put into a bad situation. If   anything, I feel bad for them. All I know is how he is with me, and he's amazing with me."

"I guess. So what was the deal with Hayden? Why was he   nervous around me?"

She laughs. "Oh, I almost forget to tell you. You have quite the reputation at the medical school." Oh shit oh shit oh shit. People know what happened. She knows what happened. She's going to be so disappointed in me.

I'm afraid of the answer. "W-what reputation?"

"Only that my pride a joy is known as a bit of an anomaly. Being so hot and the number one student in her medical school class. It's apparently a very unlikely combination." Fucking phew. I thought that was going a different way.

"Whatever. My looks shouldn't matter. I worked the hardest of anyone in my class, and people always have to mention my looks. Sometimes it hurts more than it helps."

"What does that mean?"

I look out the window. "Nothing. I'd just rather be judged on my brains. I didn't work my ass off my whole life for nothing. My looks shouldn't matter."

"Are you okay?"

"Yep. Just a bit of a sore spot for me."

"Something I should know?"

"No, not at all." Maybe I should tell her.

"I'm so incredibly proud of you." Nope. Not telling her.

Darian

What a relief that the kids all seemed to get along. I return to Jackson's that evening. He felt the same.

For the next few weeks, we spend just about every night at either his place or mine. Sometimes we have dinner together, and sometimes we meet up after our other plans, like my Sunday night dinners with my girls. But we're together every night.

When we're in bed one Friday night in our post-orgasmic haze, I turn to him and say, "I think I know what I want to check off on my fantasy list".

"Do tell. I may need a few minutes to recover," he looks down below his waist, "but I'm game for whatever you want to do." He's cute. His turnaround time is pretty remarkable, but that's not where my mind is right now.

I'm laying on him with my chin on his chest. I look up at him. "I want to go to a voyeur club with you. It's called Club Yeur."

He looks shocked. "You want people to watch us having sex?"

"No, Jackson. I don't need to have anyone watching us." I kiss my way up his chest to his lips and whisper into them, "I want you to fuck me while we watch other people having sex".

CHAPTER 15

Darian

"I can't believe we're doing this." We're in the car on our way to Club Yeur. Cassandra gave me the low down on how it all works at the club. I'm in a short, flowy, off-the-shoulder black dress. I figured it will be easy access for Jackson. Though he almost accessed me when he picked me up. I told him to save it for the club. He's in black jeans that are tight around his thick quads, and a thin white sweater stretched across his broad chest. He looks completely delicious.

"Just last night you said this is what you wanted. I want to make your fantasies come true." He picks up my hand and kisses it.

"Do you want to do it?"

"I probably could have lived my life without it, but I want to make you happy, and the more I've been thinking about it all day, the more I'm into it. I've been hard all day thinking about it."

He smiles at me. "If you wanted people to watch

us, I would have probably been a no, but I don't mind watching and doing our own thing behind closed doors. It's hot. I just don't want anyone else to see you. Your perfect body, Darian, is for my eyes only." There was something really sexy about the way he said that.

"Agree. I wouldn't want people watching us. Beyond what they already saw on the dancefloor last month." We both laugh.

Jackson

We arrive at the club. They review the options with us. Cassandra had prepared Darian for this part. We tell them we want to watch another couple, but we don't want to be watched. We want our own private, dark area where we can't be seen or heard. They ask us if we want the video package. I don't need that, but this is her picnic. I turn to her. She looks at me like I have three eyes. "No, I will definitely keep this up here." She points to her head. Me too.

She looks edible in a small black number. I wanted her the second I saw her. She had to fight me off. I'm glad she did. It only amps things up for being here.

They tell us it will be about an hour before our arrangements are ready. They'll buzz us when it's our turn. They encourage us to sit in the bar area. We sit on a sofa   together and have a few drinks.

I can't keep my hands off of her. She's so hot. Her hands are on my thighs and my dick is already hard as a rock. I need to be inside of her. When is this damn buzzer going off? She smiles looking down at my pants knowing what's going on, and what I'm thinking. She runs her tongue along my   bottom lip and whispers. "I feel the same way, Knight."

"Easier for you to hide." I put my hand under her dress.   "Perhaps I should reach in and check how my girl is feeling." She stops my hand with hers and kisses me.

"Soon enough. It will be worth the wait." She bites my lip. "I promise." She not so subtly rubs my dick as she pulls from the kiss.

She goes to pull her hand away, but I hold it there, desperate for her touch. With my other hand, I grab the back of her hair, gently pulling it to keep her close. I look at her in the eyes. "You're playing with fire." I kiss her lips hard, and then slowly move down her chin and neck, eventually landing in her cleavage. She lets out a moan.

Just then we're interrupted by the waitress with another round of drinks. We reluctantly pull apart and grab our drinks to toast the evening, a new adventure for both of us. We're approached by at least four other couples asking if we want to either watch one another fuck or swap partners. We politely decline. This wait is killing both of us. After a few more moments, I put my drink down and move my hand up her thigh again. This time she doesn't stop me. I move it under her short little dress. I can feel the outside of her underwear. She's soaking wet.

I pull in close and whisper in her ear. "Darian, look around. Look at all the men staring at my beautiful girl. All these guys here want you, but you're mine." With my fingers, I apply some pressure to her pussy. "This is mine. I'm going to make you come so hard tonight, sugar."

She lets out a loud moan. She rubs her body up and down my hand seeking some relief. She runs her hands up my chest. She can't take it anymore and climbs on top of me. "Yes, Jackson, I'm yours. And I need you now. I can't wait. I don't care who can see us." She grinds into me.

I'm about to go demand a room when our buzzer finally goes off. We look at each other and head up to the desk.

We're shown to a private room with a sectional sofa and a coffee table. I think it's supposed to look like you're in your own living room. It's got a one-way mirror, meaning we can see into the adjoining room, but they can't see us. It's dark in the other room right now. I close the door and lock it. Darian looks a little nervous. I tilt her chin up to me. "Are you okay?" She nods. "We can stop and leave whenever you want. Just say the word."

She smiles at me. "I know, but thank you for saying that. I'm good though. Just some first-time nerves, I guess. I want this. I want you." She wraps her arms around my neck and kisses me.

After a few moments, we break apart. "Let's just sit down and relax for a minute before things get started. We'll get comfortable." I place our drinks on the table.

I sit in the corner of the sofa so that my legs are completely on the sofa, but I am facing the glass so I can see in. I motion for her to come sit between my legs with her back to me, so she's facing the other room as well.

She sits down and leans back against my chest. I massage her shoulders for her, peppering her neck with kisses. I feel her begin to relax into me.

She lays her head back on my chest and starts to grind her ass onto my dick. Just then, a dim light goes on in the room we're watching. A young attractive couple comes in.

The other room is set up like a bedroom. The other couple moves towards the bed and begins to kiss pretty aggressively. Their hands are all over one another.

I can feel Darian's breathing begin to pick up, as her chest rises and falls more rapidly. Watching them is definitely turning her on. It's certainly a turn-on to watch them go at it, but watching Darian get turned on by watching them, is what gets me really going.

I rub my fingers up and down her arms, eventually moving onto her legs. Up and down. Side to side. Slow teasing strokes over her thighs.

I can feel her squirming, as her panting increases. I continue to kiss and lick her neck. The other couple begins to undress. Darian spreads her legs a bit and puts her hands on top of mine guiding them higher and higher. "Jackson," she breathes out, "please touch me. I need you to touch me."

I pull her dress up the short distance needed to get it above her lace underwear. As I slowly move my hand up, I can feel the heat emanating from her. She's on fire right now.

I reach into the top of her underwear and slip my hand down inside the front and through her lips. She moans. She's   soaking wet already.

With my other hand, I slip it down the top of her dress and under her bra. I begin to play with her nipple. I know that drives her wild. I move in slow circles around her bundle of nerves while squeezing her nipple hard. She arches her back.

The other couple is completely naked now and he's going down on her. Darian's eyes are glued to them. She's writhing, already close to her first orgasm. I stick two fingers inside of her while circling her clit with my thumb. "Oh God, Jackson. Don't stop."

I can feel her telltale spasms begin. I whisper in her ear, "come for me, sugar. All over my fingers." At my words, she convulses into her orgasm, bucking her hips, moaning my name.

After helping her ride out the orgasm, I run my drenched fingers up her body and offer them to her at her mouth. She grabs my wrist, gives my fingers one slow lick, and then slips my fingers into my own mouth. I happily oblige and slowly suck them, closing my eyes in ecstasy. "You taste so good."

Once she comes down a bit from her orgasm high, she stands up, grabs the bottom of her dress, and pulls it over her head, throwing it to the other side of the couch.

She's standing there in her black lace thong, and a strapless black bra. She's breathtaking. I am so lucky that she's mine.

She straddles her long legs around me and then slowly removes her bra right in front of my eyes, throwing it on top of her dress. Her massive breasts spill out. I stare at them salivating. They're so perfect. They're close to my face, and I stick out my tongue to flick her nipple.

I grab her breasts and start to play with them, alternating my mouth on each in slow sucking circles around her nipples.

She lets me have my fun for a few minutes before she grabs for my sweater, and pulls it over my head.

She stares at my body, running her hands up and down my chest and stomach. "Jackson, you are such a beautiful man." She moves her head down to kiss me. I can hear the other couple moaning, but I don't really even care what they're doing at this point. I'm loving the feel of Darian's chest pressed against mine as we kiss. I run my hands up and down her smooth, soft back.

She starts to move down my body and undoes my belt and zipper, occasionally peaking at the other couple. She pulls off my pants and boxer briefs.

She puts her hand around my cock and starts to pump it. I see she's about to feed it in her mouth when I grab her chin and move her eyes to mine. "Darian, tonight is about you and your pleasure. This is your fantasy. Let me pleasure you."

She smiles at me and kisses her way back up my body. When she reaches my ear, she whispers into it. "Jackson, do you enjoy tasting me?" She licks and softly bites my earlobe as I nod yes.

"Does licking my pussy give you pleasure?" Again, she licks and softly bites my earlobe as I nod yes.

"Well, I enjoy tasting you too. It gives me *great* pleasure to suck your big cock." She continues to whisper in my ear, "and now I'm going to prove it to you."

I have no idea what she's about to do. She stands up and removes her underwear. She motions for me to slide all the way down so I'm lying flat.

She turns to look at the other couple. I glance up. The woman is now riding the man. I can see the effect it has on Darian. Her eyes are full of lust. She's loving watching them.

She turns back to me and climbs over me, positioning her knees on either side of my head, with her front facing down on my body. She can see the other couple while we're like this, but I can't. I can only see her in all her glory.

She bends forward and grabs my dick. I go to put my hands on her ass and pull her down to me. She reaches back and slaps my hand away. "Not yet, Jackson. No touching. First, you're going to watch up close what me sucking your cock does to me. Pay close attention."

She grabs my dick again and licks my pre-ejaculate, which is now oozing. She circles the tip with her tongue for a moment, before taking the whole thing straight into her mouth. She's licking it, sucking it, taking it deep down her throat. It feels amazing.

I look up at her pink pussy. I can see it pulsating. The moisture is pooling. I can physically see how turned on sucking my cock makes her. This is the most erotic thing I've ever witnessed. I can't take it anymore. I need to touch her. "Darian! I need to taste you. Now."

She stops what she's doing and lifts her head. "Can you see the pleasure sucking your cock gives me? Can you see it, Jackson?"

"Yes, I see it. I need it on my mouth. On my tongue." I can sense her smile.

She spreads her knees a bit more so that her pussy moves closer to my mouth, giving me the permission I need.

She goes back to put my cock in her mouth, while I grab her ass and smash her pussy to my mouth. We're both working each other over. Both moaning in the pleasure we're giving one another.

I can hear the other couple still going at it, but I can't see. Darian lifts her head every now and then to watch them. I can tell that Darian is getting close again.

I'm trying to hold off my own orgasm, but she's making it very hard. She's sucking me so hard, and so deep down her throat. It feels so good.

I suck on her clit and slip two fingers inside her. I can feel her walls quivering. She's moaning on my cock. A few more pumps in and out, and I feel her walls squeeze my fingers hard, as her orgasm hits her.

God, I love her body's reaction to orgasms. Especially when my dick is in there for it. That will happen soon enough though.

Once her orgasm has passed, I pull her off me before I come. I'm close, but I don't want this to end quite yet. I slide up onto my knees, with her on her knees in front of me. Her back to my front. I grab her chin hard and jerk it back to me. "Did you get your pleasure, Darian?"

"Yes," she breathes. I kiss her hard.

I jerk her head back so she can see the other couple. "Do you like watching them?"

"Yes."

"Do you think she's beautiful?"

"Yes."

I bring her head back to mine and look at her in the eyes. "She's got nothing on you, Darian. Her beauty pales in   comparison to yours. I don't even see her. I only see you. Do you understand?" She nods. "Has watching them brought you pleasure?" She nods again.

"Do you want more pleasure?" I kiss her hard again.

"Yes. Please." She's out of breath from the kiss and her   desire.

"Please what? What do you want? What would give you pleasure now, Darian?"

"Fuck me, Jackson. Fuck me hard." I kiss her hard one more time. Then I bend her back over and shove her head into the couch. I grab her hips and impale her in one hard push.

She screams out. I give her a few seconds of moving slowly, as she acclimates to me, before driving hard into her. I can hear the other couple in their final shouts of orgasm, but I really don't care about them.

I dig my fingers into her hips and pump into her at a hard, fast pace. She yells out, "ah, Jackson. Oh God. So good. Keep going." I'm squeezing her hips so tightly, no doubt I'm   leaving bruises as I piston into her. Harder and harder. Stroke after stroke. We're both covered in sweat.

I reach around with one hand and pinch her clit. I feel her start to convulse, as she screams out her orgasm. Her walls are squeezing my dick so hard that I feel like I might get stuck in there. I've never felt anything so perfect. I grunt her name as I come harder than I think I've ever come before in my entire life.

We stay frozen, panting for a few moments as we come down from our collective high. I slowly pull out of her and turn her around. I lay down, pulling her on top of me with her chest to mine. I kiss the top of her head and stroke her hair. She lifelessly lies on my chest, completed sated. We lay in silence until our breathing evens out. The other couple is gone. "I think we outlasted them."

She giggles. "I guess we did. I didn't even see them finish and leave. I had a certain someone trying to kill me." She giggles again.

"I didn't hear you complaining. Just the

opposite."

She looks up at me and moves up a few inches to meet my mouth. She gives me a soft kiss. "No complaints, Knight."

I look down her body and see marks on her hips. That will definitely bruise. I cringe. I rub my hands over it to soothe it. "I hope I didn't hurt you."

"Jackson, you did a lot of things for me and to me tonight. I promise you that none of them hurt me. Just the opposite. Thank you for doing this. You exceeded the fantasy. It was amazing." She kisses me again.

We take our time, but eventually get dressed and head out.

CHAPTER 16

Darian

When my girls head to the bar for their weekly sisterly lemon drop shots at our family dinner on Sunday night, I tell Cassandra to stay put. As soon as they're out of earshot, I grab her arm. "Holy fuck, Cass, Club Yeur was insane."

She has a devious smile. "I told you. It's so hot, isn't it? Tell me what you guys did."

"We had a private room and watched another couple have sex while we had sex. The whole thing was such a turn-on. The atmosphere of the club, watching the other people, the danger of being seen, and of course, Jackson is just the icing on my fantasy cake. He literally fucked me into near unconsciousness. It was so good." I shiver at the memory of it all. "We had an amazing time."

"Good. I'm glad you pushed yourself out of your comfort zone. It's very empowering."

"It is, but you and your big mouth cannot

mention this to my girls. I'm pretty open with them, but I don't want them to know about this.

"Of course. I get that. I'm not a complete idiot. Did you get the video?"

"No, I don't get off on that like you do. I have it stored up here," pointing to my head. "That's enough for me."

"You're missing out. Memories fade. Videos last forever." That's a no for me.

"By the way, I just learned that my building is having some maintenance done over the holidays. I don't know the exact days yet. Can I stay at your house? I hate when those guys are in and out of my condo. I'd rather not be there. I should know the exact days in a few weeks when it gets closer."

"Of course. You don't even need to ask. Just come whenever you need. Jackson actually asked me to spend the New Year in Colorado meeting some of his friends, and his father, so we may fly out there after Christmas anyway."

"Wow, that's a pretty big step."

"I guess. He'll meet my parents at Christmas."

"You're officially the planning ahead couple."

"Whatever. We're enjoying the moment. Neither of us sees any reason it will stop any time soon."

Jackson

It's Monday morning. What a weekend. Saturday night was amazing. Darian was fire. I love her adventurous, naughty side. Actually, I love all of her sides and everything about her. I've never felt this way about anyone before. I think I'm in love with her, but she's not quite ready to hear that. I'm staring into space thinking of Darian when Donna buzzes me. "Yes, Donna."

"Adolf Hitler is here to see you."

"What?"

I hear her talking to someone away from the phone. "Oh, you said your name was Bryan Clarrett. I'm sorry, I thought you said Adolf Hitler." I chuckle. I love Donna. "Mr. Knight, Mr. Clarrett is here to see you."

"Tell him that I'm busy moisturizing."

I hear Bryan yelling. "I can hear you prick. Trust me, you're going to want to hear what I have to say."

"Ugh. Fine. Let him in. Have security on stand-by."

The severely out-of-shape slimeball walks into my office and plops down in a chair. With the way this guy sweats by merely sitting, I may have to replace the chair. Donna offers him a glass of cyanide, and he tells her to fuck off. She laughs and closes the door behind her on her way out.

"What do you want, Clarrett? I have a pedicure in ten minutes."

"You're hysterical, Knight. You won't be laughing when you hear what I have to say."

"Have at it. I can't wait."

"Are you still moving forward with donating the properties around the Megaplex to the government for low-income housing?" I guess he found out what I'm doing with the properties.

"Yes, would you like to donate? It's a very worthy cause."

"No, I would not." He wipes his sweaty brow and then smiles at me. "How's the hot piece of ass you've been parading around town with for the past few months?"

"She's none of your business. Stay away from her." Where is he going with this?

"Did you know that I developed most of the

properties on Monroe Street?"

"Congratulations. You turned a shitty neighborhood into a seedy neighborhood. You must be very proud."

"There's one property in particular in which I maintain an active ownership and management role. You may have heard of it. It's called Club Yeur." Shit. This can't be good. "I was there on Saturday night, and to my surprise, a certain squeaky clean respected businessman walked in along with his equally squeaky clean lawyer girlfriend. Let me assure you, they're not so squeaky clean. In fact, they're pretty filthy if you ask me."

"What we do in our private time is our business. We're allowed to go to a club. What is it you're getting at?"

"You and your girl get a little freaky in there?"

"I'm about three seconds away from putting my fist in your face."

"Did you know we have video functionality in the private rooms?"

"How wonderful for you. I would personally never disrespect my partner and utilize something like that."

"Don't worry, when I saw you come in, I turned

it on for you." He holds up a flash drive. Oh my God. He has us on video.

"You have one week to kill the low-income housing deal. Otherwise, I release the video and your girl becomes an   unwilling porn star." He starts to get up and leave. Before he passes through the door, he turns around and throws me the flash drive. "Don't worry. I have plenty of copies."

I stare out the window in stunned silence. I could care less about this video as it pertains to me, but I can't let this   happen to Darian. It would humiliate her. Her daughters would see it. Ugh. What a disaster.

I don't know what to do. My head is spinning. Should I tell her? If it were any other deal, I would just kill it. But I don't think I can kill this one. The donation paperwork has been filed to transfer ownership to the state government. It would hurt so many people if I were to kill it. I don't think I'm even legally allowed to withdraw it if I wanted to.

I don't know how to handle this. I get up and walk out my door, telling Donna that I'm not feeling well and leaving for the day. I head home, picking up several bottles of whiskey on the way. We won't get through this. She's going to blame me. I'm going to lose her.

Darian

I haven't heard from Jackson in two days. It's very unlike him. He barely goes two hours without texting me, let alone two days. We haven't gone two nights sleeping without one another in several weeks. I've sent texts and left voicemails. There's been no response. Something is wrong.

I decide to call his office and Donna answers. "Hey Donna, it's Jackson's friend Darian."

"Hey dear. How lovely to hear from you. What can I help you with?"

"Can I speak with Jackson? Is he there?"

"I'm afraid he's been out sick the past few days. He didn't tell you?"

"No, I haven't been able to get a hold of him. No worries. I'll just bring some soup to his house and check in on him." I feel a lot better knowing he's sick, and that's why I haven't heard from him. I'm not sure why he wouldn't just tell me though.

"Okay, dear. Tell him to feel better. It must be pretty bad   because he hasn't even checked in here." That's weird.

"I will. Thanks, Donna."

I pick up some chicken noodle soup from the local deli and head toward Jackson's house. When I arrive, I ring the doorbell, but no one answers. He's probably in bed sleeping. I have the code. I'll just go in.

As I walk into the main living area, I'm in shock at what I see. It's trashed. And it smells horrible. There are whiskey bottles everywhere. It looks like a frat house on a Sunday morning.

There, passed out on the floor in his boxer shorts, with an empty bottle of whiskey in his hand, is Jackson. I run over to him. "Jackson! Jackson! Wake up!" Nothing. I have tears streaming down my face. This is how I found Scott.

I lean down to feel his neck for a heartbeat. As soon as I do, his arms wrap around me. His eyes are still closed, but his arms squeeze me tight. "Yum, I smell Darian. She smells so yummy. I have a secret. But don't tell her. I love her so much, but she's going to hate me soon. She's going to leave me when she finds out." What is he talking about? At least he's alive. Barely.

I shake him hard. "Jackson, wake up!"

He opens his eyes. They're glassy. "Hey bootyful. Whas you doon heeeere?" He's smashed. I've never seen him smashed.

"Come on. You stink. Let's get you in the shower and try to sober you up." I somehow manage to get him up. His arm is hanging lifelessly around me as I struggle to move him   towards his bedroom and the shower.

He kisses my cheek. "Darian, you're the prettiest girl I've ever seen." He grabs one of my boobs. "With the best tits in the world. I want to live in them."

"Okay Romeo, let's get you undressed and in the shower."

"Only if you get undressed with me, sexy." He starts to pull up my shirt. I pull it back down and roll my eyes. He's a mess.

I manage to get his clothes off and get him in the shower. He curls up on the floor of the shower. I grab the handheld and shoot him with cold water. After about twenty minutes of that, I help him into bed. He's spread out naked on top of the covers. Just before he passes out, he mumbles, "I love you,   Darian. Please don't leave me. It's all my fault. I'm sorry." He then passes out. What the hell is going on?

I spend the next few hours cleaning up his house. It was a total mess. I start the coffee machine, and a little while later he comes down in his boxer briefs and a t-shirt. His hair is   sticking up all over the place, but he otherwise looks much better. I hand him a large cup of coffee, as he sits at the kitchen table. I give him a few sips before I break the silence. "Jackson, what's going on?"

"What do you mean?"

"What do I mean?" I'm getting mad. "You go radio silent for two days. I come here to see that you've gone through enough whiskey to service Cover Me for the next year. You're passed out cold on the floor in the middle of the day, rambling about how I'm going to leave you when I find out."

He covers his mouth with his hand. "Is that what I said? Did I say anything else?"

"Nothing else that matters right this minute."

"Oh."

"Oh? That's all you have to say? Jackson, if you slept with someone else you need to tell me."

"What? No. I would never cheat on you. I have no interest in any other women."

"Then what's going on? Why would I leave you?"

He runs his hands through his hair. "Please hear me out before you go crazy." I nod. I'm scared about whatever he's going to say. "Do you remember that jerk that hit on you a few months ago at the Children's Hospital event?"

"I think so. Ryan?"

"Bryan. Wel,l he and I kind of have a lot of bad blood between us."

"So I gathered."

"It started when we were both young in this business, and I was having success where he wasn't. His own father picked me over him to be his successor, and even though I turned him down, Bryan has never forgotten it. We've crossed paths a few times over the years, and it's always rather ugly."

"What does this have to do with me and leaving you?"

"I'm getting there. Anyway, he has a property in West Philly that he's been developing. I own several of the properties surrounding it. I ended up deciding to donate all of those particular properties to the government for them to turn into low-income housing."

"Why would I be upset about that? That's a wonderful thing to do, Jackson."

"Yes, it's great for the community, and I actually receive a lot of tax incentives for doing it. It's a win-win. It is, however, really bad for Bryan's property value, and the businesses he has as tenants. He threatened me a few months ago, and his son even threatened Trevor, but I've never taken his threats seriously."

"Until now." I nod in understanding. He's obviously holding something substantial over Jackson's head.

"Yes, until now." He takes a deep breath. "He developed Club Yeur, and maintained an ownership stake. He saw us there on Saturday night."

"Oh. Well, so what? We're entitled to be there. Who cares if he knows we went there? We're two consenting adults."

Jackson closes his eyes like he's bracing for impact. "He has access to the cameras. He turned them on in our room and   recorded us."

All of the blood drains from my face. I cover my head with my hand. "Oh. My. God." I know where this is headed now. "What exactly has he threatened?"

"That if I don't redirect the sale of those properties, he will   release the video online. I'm so sorry, Darian. This is all my fault. I'm constantly poking the bear. It was only a matter of time before he broke, and did something like this. It's all my fault." His head is in his hands and he keeps repeating that it's all his fault.

I try to remain calm. "Can you redirect the sale?"

"I suppose I can call and ask, but the paperwork is already filed and ...."

"And hundreds of people will lose their subsidized housing. We can't do that." This is a disaster.

"Not hundreds, Darian. Thousands. I don't know what to do."

"So your answer was to drink yourself into an oblivion?"

"I'm sorry. I freaked out. I don't want you to hate me. You're the best thing that's ever happened to me. My head immediately went to losing you. I've never had so much to lose."

"I don't hate you. I'm certainly not thrilled with this situation, or how you've handled it, but I don't hate you. As for losing me, let's get through this and talk further about us when we're through it."

I take a long breath. Internally I'm freaking out too, but I'm not going to go there. It doesn't help. The proof is sitting in front of me. "Jackson, you've only seen Darian the lover, Darian the mother, and Darian the fun girlfriend. You're about to see   Darian the lawyer. Buckle up buttercup." If nothing else, it gets me a smile from him.

I pull out my phone and text the number of the one person that I know can help.

Me: I need you. Code Red. I'm at Jackson's.

Crazy Cassandra: See you in 20 minutes.

Cassandra arrives eighteen minutes later. I fill her in on all of the details, leaving nothing out. "So let me get this straight, Dare. This guy recorded you without your permission, which is illegal. He's is blackmailing you, which is illegal. He's extorting you, which is also illegal. And he has a financial interest in a club that illegally recorded you, that you could sue for breach of contract and invasion of privacy. I don't see a fucking problem here. You have all the leverage, not him."

She's right. Jackson looks confused. I see where Cass is headed, but Jackson doesn't. "What do you mean he doesn't have leverage? He has a video and Darian and me doing some pretty dirty shit."

"I think I'll need to see this video to continue further discussing the situation."

I hit the table with my hand. "Cass! Focus! You do not need to see the video!"

"Can't blame a girl for trying." She winks. "Who cares if he releases the video?"

"I won't have Darian disrespected in that manner."

"No offense you two, I think you're both hot as hell, but you're not exactly Pamala Anderson in the '90's or a Kardashian. It's not like there's a huge market for videos of non-celebrity fifty-year-olds bumping uglies. Obviously, I would watch it, but I might be the only one. It's not like any of your kids are going to want to watch it, and those are probably the only people you actually really care about seeing it. Newsflash, your kids know you have sex."

I look at Jackson. "She's not wrong." Looking back at Cassandra I smile. "But it's not even going to get that far, right Cass?" It's my turn to wink at her.

"Now you see it." She has a big, devious smile.

"Cass, you're an evil genius." She continues smiling. "Jackson, invite this Mr. Clarrett to your office tomorrow morning. We're going to have a chat with him."

Cassandra high-fives me. "It's so hot when you go all badass bitch, Dare. Maybe I should hold onto the flash drive for   safekeeping." Even Jackson rolls his eyes this time, as he   purposefully bangs his head down on the table.

Jackson

On Monday morning, Donna buzzes my office at 10:00 AM on the nose. "Mr. Knight, a Joseph Stalin is here to see you." I hear commotion and yelling in the background. "Oh, I mean a Mr. Bryan Clarrett is here to see you. My mistake"

"Send him in. Thank you, Donna."

Bryan walks in with a smug expression. I motion to a chair. "Please sit, Bryan."

He sits down. "You redirect those properties, Knight?"

"No, I would never jeopardize the potential homes of   thousands of under-privileged families. It's a shame that you would."

"I'm going to release that video."

"If you must. Go ahead. I think it shows my good side."

Just then Darian walks in, looking like the sexy lawyer she is, in a form-fitting skirt suit. "*Honeybuns*, you don't have a bad side."

"Aww. Neither do you, *sweetpea*." I take her hand in mine and kiss it.

"I see you told her, Knight. That was stupid."

"I don't keep secrets from the people I care about, and I care *a lot* about Darian here."

She kisses me hard and then turns to Bryan. "Mr. Clarrett, do you know that I'm an attorney?"

"I do. So what?"

"Did you know that attorneys actually *know* the law?" He just stares at her without any response.

"Allow me the educate you a bit. Pennsylvania is a two-party consent state with regard to recordings. Being that we didn't consent to being recorded, that makes it a felony, which carries a prison term of two years. Did you know that blackmail and extortion are also felonies in Pennsylvania? They carry seven-year prison sentences. And if it's in the case of sexual extortion, which this is, the sentence can be enhanced." She turns and air kisses me.

"Oh, and Mr. Clarrett, I understand you have an ownership interest in Club Yeur. We have an air-tight civil case for invasion of privacy and breach of contract. I looked it up, being a lawyer and all, and the last case like this garnered a ten million dollar verdict."

Bryan's eyes practically pop out of his head. I lean on my desk and wrap my arms around Darian from behind. "I'm a lucky guy, aren't I Bryan?" I grin at him.

She leans the back of her body into the front of mine. "Now Mr. Clarrett, here's what's going to happen. You will get Jackson all remaining recordings of us. Every single flash drive, computer file, disk or otherwise. You will erase any and all evidence of this recording from your hard drives. You will also sign a notarized document confirming that we have all copies in existence *and* that you have committed the crimes I've laid out for you today."

"You're crazy, lady. Why would I ever do that?"

"Well, we can call the police now and let them sort it out. Or you can give us what we want, and run along with your mundane life. It's your choice. Make no mistake, there are only two options."

Bryan stands to leave. "You two crazy motherfuckers   deserve each other. Send me the damn paperwork." With that, he walks out the door and slams it behind him.

We stay as we were for a moment. Me leaning on my desk. Her back to my front. My arms around her. Seeing her like that was a huge turn-on. I can feel myself hardening. She must feel it too because pushes her ass onto me, only making me harder.

I move my hands to her breasts and grab them. I kiss up her neck and whisper into her ear. "Watching you like that was so fucking hot."

I go back to kissing her neck as I open her suit jacket. I pull her bra down and grab her perfect tits. She reaches back and grabs my erection, rubbing it up and down. I move my hands down the sides of her body to the bottom of her skirt and lift it up to her waist. I run my hands all over her thighs, higher then lower in a teasing pattern, as she continues to rub me.

I eventually work my way up to her thong and tear it from her body. She turns around, throws her arms around my neck, and starts kissing me. I quickly start walking us to the wall, me walking forward and her backward. I'm unbuckling my belt and unzipping my pants as we go. I pull out my cock.

We reach the wall, with Darian's back to it. She momentarily breaks the kiss. "Fuck me now, Jackson."

I grab her legs, she wraps them around my waist, and I slam into her. "Oh, God Jackson. That feels so good. It's been so long." It's been three days.

I give her a few moments to acclimate to me.

She yells "go". I start pumping into her at a rapid pace. Her eyes roll into the back of her head. She's moaning so loudly. No doubt poor Donna can hear us.

I try to kiss away her moans, but it doesn't work. She's in another world right now, and I've never seen anything so sexy. I'm working us both into a frenzy. My office is practically shaking.

I bend my head down and bite her nipple. "Jackson, it's too good. I'm going to come." I feel her squeezing my dick as her orgasm rips through her. It's such an indescribable feeling. I can't last and pump her a few more times before I grunt through my own release.

I give her a slow, lazy kiss as we both come down from our post-orgasmic bliss. She pulls her legs down to the ground and then pulls her skirt down. She silently goes to the   bathroom to clean up. I tuck myself back in my pants, refastening the button and my belt.

When she returns from the bathroom, she turns to me. "I'll send you the contract for Clarrett to sign. Please make sure it gets done. I'd like all of the copies of the video." I nod as she walks out the door and out of my life.

CHAPTER 17

Darian

It's been two weeks since I walked out of Jackson's office. Two weeks since I've spoken to him or seen him. It feels like two years. He sent me the signed document and all of the copies of the video. He calls and texts everyday asking to talk to me. I ignore him. I know I need to talk to him eventually, but I'm just not ready to do it yet. I'm so mad at him. His reaction to the blackmail was completely ridiculous. Ignoring the problem and drinking. Not talking to me. Hurting himself. I just can't seem to get past it.

We promised each other that we'd be straightforward. There'd be no immature nonsense. He broke those promises. Cassandra thinks I'm overreacting. She doesn't understand that finding him passed out on the floor did something to me. I think I flashed back to finding Scott on the floor, and the feeling that my world was ending came flooding back as if no time had passed.

When Jackson was drunk, he told me that he was in love with me. I think I'm in love with him too, but I'm confused. How can I love someone that isn't Scott? I'm not sure I can let myself love and lose again. It's too damn painful. This situation is a reminder of that.

I'm holed up in my room again, just like I was after Scott died. My girls are worried about me. They constantly call to check-in. They don't know exactly what happened, just that   something did happen to cause us to break up. Tomorrow is Thanksgiving. I've got to start cooking. I can't seem to do it though. I can't find the motivation. I don't think I've showered in a few days. I'm officially a disaster.

I hear the front door open. I really don't want any company right now. "Mom, are you here?" It's Harley. She walks into my room and sees me curled up on my bed. "Mom, you're a disgusting mess."

"Lovely to see you too, honey."

"I'm not letting you get away with this self-loathing again. You can't stay in this bed all day every day. I brought someone with me." Jackson walks into my bedroom with his head down. He looks as bad as I do. Maybe even worse.

"I'm locking you two in here until you work it out. Whatever it is, kiss and make up. You're both miserable. The six of us can't take it anymore. And a shower wouldn't kill either of you." She closes the door. A few moments later I hear my front door close as well.

He slowly takes off his shoes and crawls into bed with me. He pulls up close behind me and wraps his arms around me. "I miss you, sugar. I need you." I miss him too. I start silently crying. I know he can feel me shaking. "Don't cry. Please. I can't stand it. What can I do to make this better?"

I'm silent for a moment before I start speaking. "You hurt me, Jackson. You promised honesty. You just disappeared on me without any explanation. What would have happened if I didn't come over that day? What if something happened to you? I couldn't have handled it. I can't lose the man I love again. I can't go through it. It would break me." I hear him gasp, and I feel him tighten his arms around me.

Oh shit. I just told him that I love him. I didn't mean to. I close my eyes in regret.

"You love me?" I don't respond for a few moments before I slowly nod my head in confirmation. He pops his head up and kisses my cheek. "I love you too."

"I know. You already told me."

"When?"

"When you were drunk. Right before you felt me up, told me how much you love my boobs and that you want to live in them."

I can feel him shaking with laughter. "It's true. I do want to live in them." He squeezes me again. "It's also true that I love you."

I sigh. The simple fact is that I do love him. I do want him in my life. "Jackson, if we're going to do this, you need to promise me that you won't disappear on me and hurt yourself again."

"I promise."

"Seeing you passed out on your floor almost destroyed me."

"I get it. I'm sorry. It will never happen again."

"Jackson?"

"Yes."

"We both smell. Let's take a shower."

I can feel him smiling. He knows he's got me. "Okay."

We get up, quietly undress one another and get in the shower. He cleans me, I clean him, and then we slowly make love and need to clean each other all over again.

It's Thanksgiving morning. Since it's only him

and his   boys, and me and my girls, which of course includes   Cassandra, we decide to consolidate and have one big Thanksgiving celebration at his house. He had hired someone to cook, and considering the emotional toll of the past few weeks on me, I'm okay just playing football, watching football on TV,   drinking wine, and relaxing by the fireplace.

We decide to switch families for the football game. I'm with his boys and he's with my girls. Cassandra prefers to cheer from the sidelines, as does Payton's wife Kylie. I hate when women sit on the sidelines. I'm proud that my girls are always willing to play, even if I get a little competitive at times.

Reagan looks at Jackson. "Have you ever seen Mom play sports? She's crazy competitive. She's going to turn this into a blood sport. Watch your back." I laugh. There may be a little truth in that statement.

Trevor high-fives me. "Don't let them get in your head, Darian. I'm happy to finally have a teammate who cares about winning as much as I do. Stay focused."

I grab the ball and start to warm up. "This is in the bag, kid."

I throw five touchdown passes to the boys, as we easily win. Jackson only seems interested in tackling me after each throw. In fact, his hands haven't left my body since he arrived at my house yesterday, and got into bed with me. Cassandra keeps shouting for us to get a room. The kids are all laughing and having a great time. This is our first laughter-filled Thanksgiving since Scott died. His absence was felt so profoundly at the last few, but today feels full of life, family and happiness again. It feels good.

We spend the rest of the afternoon being lazy on the couch, watching the football games. Jackson and I are cuddled up in the corner. I'm pretty sure that Trevor has been coming on to Cassandra. She's eating it up.

During one of the football games we're watching, a guy   proposes to his girlfriend, and they show it on the screen.   Reagan scrunches up her nose. "That is so cheesy. Ugh, I would say no if a guy ever asked me like that at a ballgame."

I laugh. "I totally agree. Who would want to get engaged in a stadium of tens of thousands of strangers?" Harley, Kylie and Skylar agree with us.

Jackson tickles me. "You guys are snobs. Do you know how much guts it takes to ask someone like that? If they say no, it will be on Sports Center for months, and likely some blooper reels for life. Those guys are really putting themselves out there." Of course Payton, Hayden and Trevor agree with him.

Once the games are over, Jackson shows my girls to the various guestrooms so that they can shower and change. I teasingly go to follow them, and he grabs me around the waist and carries me into his room like a caveman. We don't surface again for over an hour. We come back out to a room full of laughter, and a round of applause from everyone. We take our bows.

We're sitting around the table eating and chatting. Trevor starts talking about romance novels. "Did you know that the number one seller in romance novels is step-sibling relationships?"

We all start cracking up. Cassandra is giggling at everything Trevor says. "Darian, I love this kid. He's hysterical. Where was he when I was in my twenties?"

He turns to her with a very serious look on his face. "Did you know the number two seller in romance novels is May   December romances with an older woman and younger man?" He blows her a kiss.

I look at Jackson. Oh boy. "I think we need to keep an eye on these two."

He smiles. "Better those two than two of our kids."

"That's very true."

Payton stands and clinks his glass with his knife. "Can I get everyone's attention? I have an announcement to make." He looks lovingly at Kylie, takes her hand in his, and kisses it. "Kylie and I are pregnant." The whole room erupts in cheers.

Kylie smiles. "I didn't realize that you are pregnant too, Payton. I must have missed it while my head has been in the toilet for the last two straight weeks." They smile at each other.

"Correction, my amazingly beautiful wife is pregnant. I'm just the lucky bastard that gets to go along for the ride." He looks down at her and lifts his eyebrows. She nods approvingly.

Jackson has a huge smile on his face and tears welling in his eyes. He's such a beautiful man. I whisper in his ear. "You're going to be a GILF." He squeezes my leg under the table and kisses my cheek.

"How far along," Skylar asks.

"Only seven weeks, but we couldn't wait to tell our families. We told mine last weekend when we visited. We're due in July."

I turn to Kylie. "Being pregnant in the summer is no joke. Trust me, I know." I look at Skylar, my summer baby. "You're going to want to live in that pool Jackson has here."

"You're welcome here anytime, Kylie," Jackson adds.

"Actually," Payton interrupts, "we're looking at houses. We found one not too far from here that has a pool. The house we grew up in had a pool, and I loved having it. Hayden, Trevor and I would swim all day long. We want that for our kids too. We put in an offer yesterday."

Jackson gets up to hug Payton. "I love that you'll be so close to me. I'd be happy to take a look at the house if you'd like." Payton nods. Jackson looks so happy and full of pride.

After the celebration dies down, we continue with our various conversations. I overhear Jackson ask Harley if she's seeing anyone.

"No, I just don't have any time to date. I'm working forty-eight-hour shifts. When I get off of work, I just want to sleep. I think this week is the first time I've worn non-scrubs in three months."

Trevor joins the conversation. "Isn't the hospital like Grey's Anatomy where everyone is getting it on in the on-call rooms?" Harley's eyes pop wide open. There's definitely   something going on there.

Hayden jumps in. "You're an idiot, Trevor. That's a TV show, not real life. That's not what goes on." He turns to Harley, "I think you're amazing. You're going to be such a great surgeon. Do you know what specialty you want yet?"

"Yes, I want to be a heart surgeon. I want to save people with bad hearts." I smile at her with emotion, knowing exactly why she wants to do that.

The rest of the evening goes off without a hitch. It's actually really nice having the help. I'm able to do nothing but relax and enjoy myself. We kick about eight bottles of wine among all of us.

Everyone is feeling good, except for Harley because she has a shift beginning at midnight. She couldn't drink at all.

Everyone eventually retires to their various rooms. Harley leaves for the hospital. I have no idea if Cassandra and Trevor stay put in their respective rooms. I don't even want to know. Jackson and I have another amazing night together, eventually falling asleep naked and sated in each other's arms. It feels   almost too perfect. That's because it is.

CHAPTER 18

Jackson

Christmas Eve rolls around. My boys are away with their mother at some luxurious beach resort in the Caribbean.

This is the worst time of year to be divorced. I want to spend the holidays with my boys. If we're both in town, we spend it all together, but some years one of us will take them on vacation. That's just the way it goes.

Fortunately, I have Darian and her family this year.   Darian's parents drove in today from Washington DC, and are staying over at her house tonight. Her brother is   spending Christmas with his wife's family, so I won't get to meet him just yet.

I'm going over to her house for Christmas Eve dinner, and to meet her parents. I'm looking forward to finally meeting them and excited for the big surprise that I have for her   entire family.

To be honest, I'm a little nervous. I haven't had to meet a girlfriend's parents in over thirty years, and that time we also told them that we were pregnant and getting   married at only nineteen years old. I imagine this will go a bit differently than me getting punched in the face by an angry father and two angry brothers. At least I hope so.

I arrive with a few good bottles of wine in my hands. Darian opens the door with a big smile on her face.

She looks gorgeous in a red wrap-around dress. She runs her arms up my chest and around my neck, and gives me a nice long kiss, as if she hasn't seen me in a month, as opposed to this morning when she left my house.

Reagan walks by. "Here we go again. You two are ridiculous. Haven't you had enough of that yet? It's like living with horny teenagers, except I don't live with you and you're not actually teenagers. Yet here I am constantly having to see it." She smiles in jest. "Nana, Poppop, come meet Jackson   before he and Mom disappear off somewhere."

Darian playfully smacks Reagan's behind. "I can still ground you. You better watch it, young lady."

Reagan   deadpans.   "I   literally   have   been

watching it. Every damn time I'm around the two of you."

Darian laughs, hands Reagan the wine I brought, and grabs my hand to lead me into the main living area. "Mom, Dad, this is Jackson Knight. Jackson, these are my parents, Charles and Anne Kaplan."

I shake her Dad's hand. "It's a pleasure to meet you, sir."

"Please call me Chuck."

"Thank you. It's a pleasure to meet you, Chuck."

I go to shake her mother's hand, but she comes in for a hug. "Nice to finally meet you, Jackson. I've heard so much about you." She breaks the hug and turns to Darian, "though Darian, sweetie, I don't think you did him any justice as to just how handsome he is."

I lift my eyebrow at Darian in question. "Don't add to his already over-inflated ego, Mother. I told you he's *fairly* attractive. Handsome may be a bit of a stretch." She smiles playfully at me.

I put my arm around Darian and squeeze her close. "That's just because everything and everyone pales in comparison to Darian's beauty." I kiss her cheek and smile proudly.

Skylar rolls her eyes. "Oh, God. Don't get them started, Nana. Just wait. We're going to have to suffer through them   making googly eyes at each other all night. They'll   practically be dry humping by dessert."

Darian scowls at Skylar. "You're all brats. Every single one of you." She motions to the dining room. "Come on, let's eat so we can get to our Christmas Eve presents. Hopefully, Harley will be here soon. She should be getting off of work right about now."

We have a nice meal. I learn all about Chuck's insurance business and golf game. I offer to take him out to play once the warmer weather returns. Anne is a bit of a golfer too. She also plays tennis and pickleball. I guess the athletic genes run strong in this family, as does beauty. Darian looks a lot like her mom.

At some point during the meal, Harley comes in. She's still in scrubs and looks exhausted. She says a few quick hellos and then goes to take a shower before joining us.

Darian brings out a variety of desserts. "Why don't we eat dessert while Harley finishes her dinner, and then we can open one present each tonight. Only one though. The rest get saved for the morning."

Darian comes over to me and sits on my lap as

we eat our dessert. Skylar nods her head in our direction. "I told you what would happen come dessert."

Darian looks at her. "Skylar, this is not dry humping. If you think it is, perhaps you and I should go in the other room and have a little chat about the birds and bees." Everyone laughs, except Skylar. She just shoots daggers at her Mom.

Harley finishes, and we all gather around the tree.   Darian did an amazing job on her tree. It looks beautiful. She   excitedly hands me a small rectangular box. I open it up and it's a Rolex watch. Wow. This is a really nice gift. She whispers for me to read the inscription. I read it out loud. "To My Favorite GILF. Always, Darian."

She quickly covers my mouth. "I didn't mean out loud,   Jackson."

Reagan starts giggling. "Oh my God. GILF. That's freakin' hysterical. Mom, you're ridiculous." Skylar and Harley just shake their heads and cover their eyes.

Anne asks, "what's a GILF?"

Harley replies, "nothing you need to worry about, Nana. Nothing you want to know about. Trust me." I love the watch. I put it on immediately.

It's my turn. I pull an envelope out of my blazer pocket and hand it to Darian. "This is actually for everyone in this room, plus Cassandra." She's not here tonight for some reason.

Darian opens it. She puts her hand over her mouth in shock. "Oh wow."

Skylar looks up. "What is it, Mom?"

"It's a VIP box for all of us for the Capitals versus the   Flyers game here in Philly tomorrow afternoon. I completely forgot that the Caps are in town tomorrow. Jackson, this is amazingly generous. Thank you."

Chuck adds, "Thank you, Jackson. I haven't been to a game in ages. You know, I used to take Darian to games all the time when she was growing up. Her brother too. They would fight like cats and dogs over who got to go to which games."

"I know, sir. Darian has told me how special it was to her to go to the Caps games with you as a kid. That's why I got these seats for everyone. So she could go with you again."

Darian comes over to me with unshed tears welling in her eyes. She grabs my cheeks and gives me a soft kiss on the lips. She whispers into them. "You're an amazing man,   Jackson Knight. I love you. Thank you for this."

Chuck interrupts our moment. "Jackson, do you know who the greatest hockey player of all time is?"

"Well, sir, I used to think it was Wayne Gretzky, but since I've started dating your daughter, I've learned that it's Alexander Ovechkin."

Chuck smiles proudly. "Damn straight it's Alexander Ovechkin. He's the best goal scorer of all time. Gretzky had it easy with small goalies compared to the monsters Ovi has had to encounter." I laugh to myself. The apple definitely doesn't fall far from the tree.

"That's what I hear."

Darian

I put on my robe and come out of my room for a glass of water at about 1:00 AM. Jackson is asleep in my bed. He didn't want to stay over out of respect for my parents, but I reminded him that we're nearly fifty years old, each have been married and each have three kids. I think that cat's officially out of the bag with my parents that we're not virgins. Besides, I really needed to thank him for that amazingly thoughtful gift. Twice.

I'm drinking my water when I hear "hello sweetie."

I startle. "Oh, hey Mom. You startled me. I didn't see you there."

"I'm sorry. I couldn't sleep. Your father is snoring. I'm   surprised you can't hear it across the house. I thought I'd come out and get some reading done." She puts her Kindle down and pats the sofa seat next to her. "Come and sit with me for a few minutes. I want to talk to you alone."

I go over and sit down. "Jackson is lovely. He seems quite   smitten with you."

I smile. "He is. I'm smitten with him too."

"I can see that. I'm so happy for you. It's been a long few years for you, Darian. I've been so worried about you. It's good to see you living your life again." She pauses for a moment. "Where do you see this relationship going? Do you think you'll get married?"

I'm surprised by the questions. "Get married? Why would we get married? We've both had all the kids we're going to have. There's no reason for us to ever get married. There's no reason for me to ever get married again. Jackson understands that my one and only husband is Scott."

"*Was* Scott. You mean Scott *was* your husband, Darian. He is not currently your husband. Your vows were until 'death do you part'. You've reached that."

I look at her like she's got three eyes. "That's not how I see it, Mom. I committed my life to him. *My* whole life. Jackson gets it. You're making an issue where none exists. We're happy as we are."

"Are you sure about that? I watched him tonight. He's very much in love with you, Darian. I'm pretty sure you're in love with him too."

"I am."

"Well in my experience, when a man looks at a woman like that, they want forever. And they want it to be official.   Jackson seems like a wonderfully sweet man who would take care of you. That's all we want. You're very young to be a widow, Darian. You have a lot of life left to live. We don't want to see you spending it alone. You need someone like Jackson by your side."

My mother can be so old school sometimes. "Mom, Jackson and I take care of each other. Despite how young I was when I   married Scott, I'm actually a pretty independent woman. While your generation may have *needed* a man, I do not. Do I *want* Jackson in my life right now? Yes, I do. Do I *need* him in my life? No, I don't. Jackson and I will continue spending time together as long as we *both* want that. Neither of us has any need for the formalities of a marriage."

She contemplates my words for a moment. "Have you two discussed this?"

"No, we don't need to. We're on the same page."

"Hmm."

"What does that mean?"

"Nothing. We'll see. Good night sweetie. See you in the morning." She gets up to head back to her room.

I mumble good night to her. Ugh. Mothers. They're always fucking with your head.

The hockey game was a blast. We got booed by the Philly fans when we showed up in our red Caps jerseys, in a sea of orange Flyers jerseys. For some reason I find upsetting Philly fans to be very exhilarating.

Ovi scored a hat trick and the Caps won the game. When the game was over, Jackson surprised us all with a short meet and greet with Ovi. We got tons of pictures with him. I don't think I've ever seen my father as happy as the moment he shook Ovi's hand. Naturally, he gushed all over Ovi, and told him that he's the greatest player of all time.

Cassandra copped a feel, so the pictures ended

rather abruptly, but we all got the photos and memories we wanted. I'm so grateful to Jackson for this special day.

Jackson

It's Friday morning and we're leaving for Colorado in a few hours. Darian is gone for her weekly visit to the cemetery. She goes every week on Friday mornings. I'm pretty sure she just talks to him about her life and the girls. I don't think the girls go with her. Perhaps they go on their own at other times. She's never spoken with me about it, other than to say that she goes to visit. I certainly don't want to pry. I can't say it doesn't bother me a little bit, but I would never say that to her. If it's what she needs to manage what she's been through, then so be it. I try not to be too insecure about it. She usually returns a little emotional. I generally give her an hour or two to herself before I speak with her. I'm usually at work when she goes anyway.

An hour after she returns, I poke my head in to see if she's ready to go to the airport. She nods her head. I can tell she's been crying, but I don't acknowledge it. I don't want to make her feel self-conscious.

We watch Wedding Crashers on the flight out. It's Darian's favorite movie, and she belly laughs the whole time.

With the time change, we land in Denver at 4:00 local time. We grab our luggage and rental car. "Let's go check into the hotel and clean up. We're having dinner at my Dad's house tonight. I thought tomorrow we could go skiing for a bit, and then tomorrow night we'll be with Will and his entire family. For New Year's Eve the following night, we'll be with just Will and Frankie at the party, sans the kids."

She looks surprised. "We're not staying with your father?"

"No, his place is kind of small. He won't let me buy him a bigger place. I want some private alone time with you   anyway, and you're kind of a screamer." I give her a big smile

She smacks my arm. "I'm not that loud."

"Yes, you are, sugar. And I absolutely love it and wouldn't want you any other way." I kiss her nose.

We check in to the hotel, quickly change and head over to my dad's house. When we walk in, my father gives me a huge hug, lifting me off the ground. He's a big guy like me. He probably had an inch on me in his heyday, but now we're about the same height. That's where our similarities end. He's light with fair skin. I look more like my mom with darker skin, jet black hair and green eyes.

"How's my boy? You look good, son. You don't age."

"I'm good, Dad. It might just be relative, being that you're getting older." He laughs. I grab Darian's hand. "Please meet the love of my life, Darian Lawrence. Darian, this is my father, Jesse Knight." Darian gives me a little bit of a look with that introduction. She tentatively moves to hug him.

"It's so nice to meet you. What would you like for me to call you?"

"It's nice to meet you too, pretty lady. You can call me Jesse... or Dad." Her eyes just about pop out of her head." I whisper to her that Jesse is fine. That puts her at ease.

"Ooh, I almost forgot. I have something for you, Jesse." Darian pulls a wrapped gift out of her purse and hands it to my father. "Merry Christmas." I didn't know she was doing that. I have no idea what it is. I give her a squeeze of thanks.

Dad opens it. It's framed picture of Payton, Trevor, Hayden and me from our football game on Thanksgiving Day. We've got our arms draped around each other with huge smiles. I haven't seen this picture. "Thank you, Darian. What a great shot of my four favorite boys. I'm going to display it front and center." He places it right in the middle of the mantle, over his fireplace.

"That was during our Thanksgiving football game. You should ask your son who the winning quarterback was." She smiles at me. "That person may have thrown five touchdown passes."

"I couldn't concentrate on the game. I was blinded by her beauty." She rolls her eyes at that, and my Dad laughs.

"I can certainly understand that, son. Come on. Let's eat. Dinner's getting cold."

We eat a nice meal with my father. He asks Darian lots of questions about her girls and her life. She asks him a lot of questions about me growing up. When she excuses herself to go to the bathroom, he leans over towards me. "You really like this girl, huh?"

"I love her. She's the one. I have no doubts about that   whatsoever."

"You need to be careful, son. Widows are a different breed. You chose to end your marriage to Melissa. It's different for widows. It's chosen for them. It's hard to ever really get over the loss. Trust me, I know firsthand." My father certainly does know firsthand. He's dated over the years, but he never remarried. He said that there's no better woman out there, so there's no need.

Darian returns and I look at my father. "Dad, do you mind if after we clear the table, I take Darian to my old treehouse? I'd like to show her your handy work."

"Of course. Don't worry about clearing. There are only three of us. I've got it. You kids go have fun. There are some   blankets on the chair over there. It's cold out. Take them with you."

"Thanks, Dad."

"Thanks for dinner Jesse. It was delicious." He smiles at her.

Darian and I grab the blankets and head out to my old tree house. It's a bit more than your run-of-the-mill treehouse, even given its age. My father was a carpenter. This thing is probably built better than most houses. We climb up and Darian looks around. "Wow, Jackson. This treehouse is nicer than an actual house."

"I know. My Dad is the best. He built houses for a living. He didn't know any differently, so this was built like one of them. Just a smaller version."

We put out the blankets and lay down. We look up at the stars. There's actually a skylight in the treehouse, so we can see the clear Colorado sky from in here. You can't see the stars like this in Philly. It's one of the things I miss most about Colorado.

Darian grabs my hand as she looks up. "What a view." I look at her. My thoughts exactly. "This treehouse must have been a chick magnet for you. You must have gotten a lot of ladies to drop their panties in here, Knight."

I laugh. "No, not at all. He built it for me when my Mom got sick so I'd have somewhere to come to do whatever I needed to do. Think, relax, cry, yell, scream. Whatever I needed to do to get through watching my Mom deteriorate the way she did."

"That's really sweet that even in his time of loss, he valued your needs so much."

"That's my Dad for you."

"So you're telling me you never had any girls in here? Not one?"

"Nope, just my place to come and be alone."

"Sort of like the jazz club. The jazz club is treehouse east for you."

I never thought of it that way. I smile at the

thought. "You're right. That's exactly what it is."

"So, if I were to say, suck your dick in here, you're telling me it would be a first for this treehouse?" She has a devious smile on her face.

I return the same smile. "I can't speak for the treehouse, but it would be a first for *me* in this treehouse."

She rolls over, positioning herself on top of me, straddling my big body. She grabs my face and starts to kiss me. It's just her lips at first until her tongue pushes into my mouth.

I slip my hands under her sweater, pull her bra down, and grab her big, perfect tits. She moans into my mouth. She's grinding onto me.

We make out like teenagers for a bit, until we're both worked up into frenzies. My dick is so hard, that it's about to bust through my jeans.

She sits up straddling me, and unzips my pants to pull them and my boxer briefs down to just below my dick. She pulls it out and starts to pump it with her hands.

I grab her. "I need to see your tits when you do this to me." She slowly pulls off her sweater, throws it to the side, and unfastens her bra and tosses that as well. It's pretty cold in here. Her nipples are hard as rocks.

I sit up with her and take her nipples into my warm mouth. One at a time I suck them. Her nipples are so sensitive. She's moaning and writhing on top of me.

She then puts her hands on my chest and pushes me back down. "Jackson, lay back and relax. This isn't about me. This is about you getting your big dick sucked in your treehouse."

She kisses her way down my chest and abs. She kisses the top of my cock, and then the rest of my cock on her way down.

She licks my balls, taking each into her mouth. Then she looks at me in the eyes and slowly licks her way back up to the top. She circles the tip with her tongue before taking me into her mouth.

Before I know it, she's on her knees, taking all of me in her mouth, all the way to her throat, while alternating licking and sucking. She's using both hands. There's not an inch of my cock not being taken care of. Her tits are hanging down. I grab them and play with her nipples. She moans into my cock. It drives me crazy when she does that. This feels so good. She's too good at this.

"Darian, I'm going to come. Let me inside you. She doesn't move. She just looks at me straight in the eyes and sucks harder. That's it. I can't hold it. My balls tighten and I blow my load into her mouth. She just keeps sucking until there's nothing left.

When she pulls away, a little more seeps out onto my   stomach. She bends back down and slowly licks it up. "Yum. You taste good, Knight."

I sit up and grab her face and kiss her hard. I can taste myself on her. "God, I love you."

"Getting a man to say he loves you right after you suck his dick is the oldest trick in the book." We both laugh.

I kiss her again. I grab her bra and sweater for her. "How about I take you back to the hotel and take care of you?"

"I like that plan, Knight. Let's go."

We say our goodbyes to my father and head for the hotel. My hand is down her pants, touching her, warming her up for the entire car ride back. She's so turned on right now. Watching her in that state drives me nuts. I'm already hard again.

We burst through the hotel door like we're going to knock it over. Our clothes are dropped on the floor quickly.

We're both naked by the time we reach the bed.

I push her down and climb on top of her. She's so worked up. I love how much sucking my cock turns her on. It's going to take me less than a minute to make her come for the first time tonight.

I immediately move down her body. I suck hard on both of her inner thighs, teasing her. She grabs fistfuls of my hair. "Please Jackson, make me come. I need to come so badly."

I get settled between her legs and throw them over my shoulders. I start with my tongue at her back entrance, as I will definitely spend some time there later. I lick my way all the way to the front. She moans.

I thrust my tongue in and out of her entrance. I can feel her walls squeezing my tongue. She's already screaming my name. I move my tongue to her clit, and suck hard. I know the second I stick my fingers in her, that will be it.

With my tongue on her clit, I slowly slide two fingers inside of her. Before I even have a chance to pump them, her walls spasm as she detonates into orgasm. Her orgasm rolls on and on, and I lick her and pump her all the way through it.

She eventually finishes, though she's still panting and out of breath. "Holy shit. That lasted forever. I was so worked up." She takes a few more heavy breaths. And looks down at me rubbing her fingertips over my face. "You're so incredibly sexy. Come kiss me."

I move my way up her body and kiss her. I love that she likes to taste herself on my tongue. It's so hot.

We kiss as I rub my cock through her drenched lips. I need to get her nice and wet for what I have planned tonight.   "Jackson, I need you inside me."

I come up to my knees and move to sit on the side of the bed, throwing my legs over. I grab her body and straddle it over mine, with her back to my front. I wrap my arm around her waist, lift her until I'm at her entrance, and then slowly slide her down onto me.

I love the first moment that I enter her. I can feel her whole body relax with pleasure, as her walls latch on to me.

Once I'm all the way in, she leans her head back against my shoulder, turns to me, and kisses my neck. "It feels so good, Jackson. You feel so good." I grab her tight and start moving her up and down.

I reach down with my other hand to where our bodies meet. She's dripping. I take some of the wetness with my fingers and move it to her back entrance to circle it. "Yes, Jackson." I penetrate her back entrance with two fingers. I'm moving her up and down on my cock with one arm and thrusting into her back entrance with the fingers of my other hand.

"Ah, Jackson. I'm going to come again."

"Let go." I feel her squeeze my dick, as she comes and screams my name. It's so hard to hold back, but I do.

As soon as her orgasm fades, I pull my fingers out, lift her up and off my cock, and slide it to the back to slowly enter her there. Eventually, I push all the way in.

She's breathing loudly. "You're so big. Give me a minute to get used to it before you start moving." I remain still inside her as I kiss her shoulder and neck.

She wiggles her ass as she loosens up, and eventually starts moaning. I know it's starting to feel good, and this is my green light. I start to move her up and down. She feels amazing.

She turns her head for me to kiss her. I do as I grab her breast and pull her even closer to me. She reaches her arm around and grabs my hair, holding my face close to hers as we kiss.

I suck on her lower lip. It drives her wild. "Your ass feels so good on my cock." She wiggles again and I nearly blow my load.

I move the hand from her breast down to her sex. I slide two fingers in and circle her clit with my thumb. "Oh God, Jackson. You're everywhere. It feels incredible. I love you." We kiss again.

We're both on sensory overload. I feel her walls starting to squeeze both my cock and my fingers. "I'm coming again. Come with me." This time I let go with her. We both moan loudly as we come together.

We're no longer moving our bodies, but we keep kissing. I whisper into her lips. "I love you too. So much."

I rub my hands up and down her body as she recovers from her orgasms. I'm in no rush for us to move. When she's able to stand, I gently guide my cock out of her.

I hold her tight from behind and whisper in her ear. "Let's take a bath." She's too spent to speak. She nods her head instead. I run the bath for us and help her in. I slide in behind her and hold her as I clean her up. After we're both clean, we just lay in there with the jets and relax as I keep my arms around her. I can't seem to stop rubbing and kissing her body though. This is my version of heaven. She's my version of heaven.

I let her sleep until 8:00 the next morning. I kiss

her awake. She smacks me away and mumbles sleepily. "Jackson, I let you fuck me every which way but sideways last night. Let me sleep in."

"When will sideways be on the menu?" She smacks me again and I laugh. "Come on, sugar. This may be our only day to ski out here. The weather is perfect. I want to get in as many runs as possible."

"Fine. Why do you have so much damn energy?" She sits up and stretches. The sheets drop and pool at her waist,   exposing her mouthwatering tits. I start to move towards them, and she puts up her hand. "Stop. I'm officially closed for business." She leans over and kisses me. "At least for a few hours." She smirks at me and heads to the bathroom.

We eventually make it to the slopes. She's a little rusty at the beginning, but then it kicks in for her, and we have a great day on the fresh Colorado powder. It feels good to be out here.

We stop and pick up a few bottles of wine on the way to Will's house. We arrive at Will's and park. The door is opened before we even knock. Will comes out and gives me a huge hug. "Jackson. I missed you, man. It's been forever." He turns to Darian. "You must be Darian. I've heard so much about you." He hugs her as well.

"Hey Will. It's so good to finally meet you.

Jackson speaks so highly of you."

"Sure he does. Come in. Everyone's waiting for you."

We start to walk inside. I notice Will has lost some weight. He was carrying a few extra pounds the last time I saw him. "How are you, buddy? You look good. Finally hitting the gym?"

"I have to keep up with you, you know, the world's most   eligible bachelor." I roll my eyes and Darian giggles.

We head inside to the kitchen and everyone is standing there. I kiss Frankie and look at the kids. "Wow, you guys have all gotten so big. Darian, let me introduce you to everyone. This beautiful woman is Will's better half, Frankie. To her left are their nineteen-year-old twins, Brandon and Brenda." Darian snaps her head to Frankie.

Frankie chimes in. "Yes, before you ask, I was a big Beverly Hills 90210 fan back in the day. Perhaps too big. Let me introduce you to my other three children. This is Dylan, Kelly and Donna."

Darian laughs. "Frankie, you and I are going to be good friends. This is the greatest thing I've ever heard in my life. I actually kind of want to call my best friend and tell her. She's going to freak out. It was her dream in college to have twins and name them Brandon and Brenda."

"Well, I guess I'm living her dream then."

Darian looks to the three younger kids. "How old are you guys?

Kelly answers. "I'm sixteen. Dylan is eighteen and Donna is fifteen."

"Wow, you guys didn't mess around."

"Actually, we did, that's why we had five kids in four years," Frankie jokes. We all laugh, except the kids.

Donna looks disgusted. "Ugh, mom. That's disgusting. We don't need to hear that."

Frankie smiles at her. "Why don't you five go make a Tik Tok or something. The four of us are going to enjoy this wine, that Uncle Jackson and Darian brought with them, before dinner. Dinner will be ready in about an hour."

Darian turns to the kids. "Are you guys big Tik Tok fans?" They all nod. "I had a feeling you might be. She reaches in her purse and pulls out five items that I have no clue what they are. The kids' faces light up. "One of my daughters owns a store called 'Tik Tok Trendy'. They sell all the latest Tik Tok trends. I thought you guys might like these." They all excitedly thank her. I just stare at her. This woman.

Will whispers in my ear, "you've got it bad." All I can do is nod.

The four of us have a blast and kick two bottles of wine before dinner even starts. We're laughing as Will and I tell stories from our childhood. Frankie has heard them all before, but Darian hasn't and they're funny as hell.

We sit down for dinner. Brandon turns to me. "Uncle   Jackson. Thank you for all of our new computers."

"No need to thank me again, Brandon. I got your text. I got all of your texts thanking me. I'm happy you guys like them."

Darian looks confused. Will notices and jumps in.   "Jackson here didn't think it was enough that he is practically paying for all of my kids to go to college. He bought them all computers for their first day of school as well."

"That's not true. I just helped contribute to what you started."

"You should check the math on that, buddy. I'm not taking credit for what you did. The kids know what's up." I'd have preferred the kids assumed that Will was paying for college for each of them. I guess they know that I am.

Darian picks up my hand and kisses it.

We finish off a great evening, tell Frankie and Will that we'll see them tomorrow night, and head back to the hotel.   During the car ride, Darian looks at me with love. "You're a good man, Jackson Knight."

"I wish he didn't tell the kids. I'd rather they think that Will is paying for college."

"That's part of what makes you so good."

"I know Will feels emasculated by it. But he can't afford it, and I don't want the kids to have to take out loans, and spend the next twenty years in debt."

"I think it's a wonderful thing you're doing. Will appreciates it. He just has integrity and doesn't want to take credit for something you did. He's a good man like you. I'm glad I got to meet him. I understand why you two are friends."

After another late night in bed, we sleep in on New Year's Eve morning. We order room service, hit the spa, and just have a lazy, relaxing day. I order Darian a few extra spa services while I take care of some things.

We get dressed for the New Year's Eve party we're   attending. I'm in a blue suit and blue shirt with no tie, waiting for Darian to come down to the lobby. She steps off the elevator in a strapless green dress that matches her eyes. It hugs her body to complete perfection. I reach for her and twirl her. "You are genuinely the most stunning woman on the planet. You take my breath away." I kiss her hand. "There is absolutely zero chance of me keeping my hands off of you tonight."

"That was my plan, Knight." She looks me up and down. "You look pretty breathtaking yourself." I softly kiss her. We head to the party. Will and Frankie are there when we arrive. We all hug hello. Darian and Frankie admire each other's dresses. I'm happy they get along so well.

At some point during dinner, Frankie and Darian head to the bathroom. This is the first time that Will and I have been alone. "Wow Jackson. I've never seen you like this."

I shrug my shoulders. "I guess love changes you. Even my old ass."

"You haven't changed. It's just that for the first time in your life that you're truly happy."

"I am happy. She's amazing."

"She's gorgeous."

"She is, but it's not just that. It's everything about her. I think I'm addicted to her." He laughs at that.

"I get it. I really do." I know that's true. He and Frankie are the real deal. "I hope it works out. I know she has some baggage."

"Nothing we can't overcome." He nods. "Remember we're heading out early."

"I remember. Good luck buddy."

The girls return. We finish our meal and spend the next few hours dancing and drinking champagne. We're having a blast. I love dancing with Darian. I love the feel of her body on mine. Being true to my word, I don't keep my hands off of her for the entire evening. Once I see that it's 11:15. I grab her hand. "Time for us to go."

"What do you mean time for us to go? It's almost midnight. Why would we leave?"

"I have plans for us, sugar. Trust me." We say our goodbyes to Frankie and Will and head out.

We get in the car. "I have no clue what you're planning, Knight. It seems strange to leave the party right before midnight."

"There's something special I want to do with you as we ring in the new year."

"We've done that something special about a hundred times this weekend."

I chuckle. "Not that. At least not until later."

We arrive at Dad's house. Darian is looking at me like I'm crazy. We bypass the front door and head towards the   backyard. I help her up into the treehouse. She walks in and looks around. The floors are completely covered with plush blankets. There are lights strung everywhere. There are lit candles on the tables and window sills. She turns around to me and finds me on one knee. Her eyes open wide and she covers her mouth.

"Darian. You came into my life and flipped it upside down. Besides my love for my children, I've never known pure, true love in my entire life. In you came and taught me what it is. I love every single thing about you, and I don't want to exist another day without it. I know without any doubt that you are the one true love of my life. You are my soulmate. You are my everything. I want you to be my wife. I want to bring in the new year with our new life together."

I pull a box out of my pocket and open it to a three-carat, square-shaped diamond ring. "Darian, will you make me the luckiest man on the planet and marry me?"

She hesitates for a moment and then she shocks me. "No."

CHAPTER 19

Darian

No, I just said no. Jackson offered me a magnificent proposal, and I said no. He stands up and puts the ring back in his pocket. I see tears in his eye. I go to approach him, but he takes a step back.

"Jackson, I'm so sorry. The proposal was beautiful. You're a beautiful man, and I do love you." I step towards him again wanting to touch him, but he holds his hand up to stop me. "I just can't get married again. I didn't realize that you wanted marriage. We've never talked about it. I thought we were on the same page."

He has his head down. He can't even look at me. "I thought we were in love."

"We are in love."

"People in love want to marry one another."

"Jackson, I pledged my love and loyalty to another man many years ago. I married him. I know he died, but I can't betray him like this. I can't marry someone else."

"Darian, you're allowed to be happy. You're allowed to   remarry."

I shake my head. "You're not understanding me."

I can see him starting to get angry. He puffs out his chest. "I'm not understanding? Are you fucking joking me? I've been nothing but understanding. I've never had a problem talking about him. I've never said anything about all of the   pictures of him hanging in your house. I've never said anything about your weekly visits. I don't complain that you hang with his high school buddies every Monday night. I've never complained about the fact that I know I will never have your whole heart. Do you comprehend how hard that is for me? I love you. You own every ounce of my heart. I have to live with the fact that even if you do love me, which I know you do, no matter what I do or how much time passes, I will never own your whole heart. You will always save a piece for him. You're the love of my life, but you'll never see me as yours. That fucking kills me. Even knowing all this, I still want you. But I won't settle for halfway. I want you in my bed every damn night. I want you living in my house. I want to wake up to your face every morning for the rest of my life. I want to make love to you every day for the rest of my life. I want you as my wife, Darian."

We're both in full-fledged tears now. This is all my fault. I'm responsible for the broken look on his face. I'm responsible for the tears in his eyes. But I can't give myself to him like that. I belong to another man. I croak out, "I'm sorry Jackson, I just can't do that to him."

We ride back to the hotel in silence. He calls and moves our flight up to first thing in the morning. He lays as far away from me as he can. I don't think either of us actually sleeps a wink though.

We fly home in silence. He drives me to my house, takes my luggage out of the car, and puts it by my front door. I touch his arm and whisper, "Jackson."

He pulls his arm away from my touch. "Please don't." He has tears in his eyes again. He can't even look at me in the eyes. "I hope you find whatever it is you're looking for." He walks away, gets in his car, and leaves.

I whisper but no one can hear, "you're what I'm looking for." I walk inside and close the door. I slide down the wall and start to cry. At some point, I take out my phone to text.

> Me: Code red. My house.

> Crazy Cassandra: I'm in your bed.

Oh right, she's staying here. I go to my room and she's laying in my bed. She sees my face and opens her arms. I lay down and sob. Gut-wrenching sobs. For over an hour I do nothing but sob. She just holds me and lets me do what I need to do. When it's clear that I have nothing left in me she pulls back. "What happened?"

"He asked me to marry him?"

"What's the problem?"

"I'm already a married woman."

She sighs. "No Dare, you're not a married woman. When you were only forty-five years old, your husband died. The day he died you stopped being a married woman. You then spent three years locked up in misery. Then this wonderful man came into your life and brought you back to life. You two are in love. I've seen it with my own eyes. There's no reason you can't get married."

"Cass, on my first date with Scott do you know what quality he told me he valued most in a partner?"

"What?"

"Loyalty. He said he valued loyalty above all other traits. I've given him loyalty every single day of our marriage. Even though I've spent time with Jackson the past few months, and I admit I have fallen in love with him, in my heart, I need to give some loyalty to Scott. I need to keep this one part just for him and no other man. He's the only man that I will ever marry. I owe this to him."

"You're playing with semantics. You don't owe this to him. You were an amazing wife to him in his life. That's what you *did* owe him. You keep his memory alive with the girls. That's what you *currently* owe him. You don't owe him anything else."

"You just don't understand. Neither does Jackson."

"I don't blame him. He's madly in love with you. You're the first woman he's ever been in love with. Can you blame him for wanting to marry you?"

"I can't talk about this anymore."

"Whatever. I'll give you a few days to wallow, and then you're going to put on your big girl pants and fix this."

"It's irretrievably broken. You didn't see his face. I broke his heart."

"I bet you did."

"The girls don't know that I'm home. We were supposed to stay out there for two more days. Please don't tell them I'm back or what happened. I need to get my shit together before I talk to them."

"Fine. I'm off work this week anyway. We can eat ice cream and watch movies. A few days though. You only get a few days."

"We'll see."

Jackson

I've been in bed for over forty-eight hours. I've never been so thankful that everyone thinks I'm away. No one has bothered me. How did I misread things so badly? I thought she loved me as I love her. I thought she wanted to spend her life with me as I do her. I was so wrong. I was just someone to pass her time. A temporary place filler.

I hear my front door open. "Dad, are you back?" It's Payton. I manage a grunt to let him know where I am. He walks into my bedroom. "What the hell? It stinks in here. You look like shit. Are you sick? Didn't you just get back this afternoon? Where's Darian?

"We came back early."

"Why?"

"She broke my heart."

"What?"

"I asked her to marry me and she said no. She doesn't love me."

"She said she doesn't love you? I doubt that."

"No, she said she loves me, but can't marry me because in her heart she's already married to another man."

"Oh." He fidgets nervously, unsure what to say. "I'm sorry Dad. I know you thought she was the one."

"She is the one. I'm just not meant to get to marry the love of my life."

He looks at me like I'm pathetic. I am pathetic. "Come on, Dad, let's get you in the shower. You'll feel better once you clean up a bit."

"Doubtful."

Darian

"Hey, baby. I haven't seen or spoken to the girls this week, so nothing to report there. It's been a rough week for me though." I sit down in the grass by his tombstone and run my fingers along the inscription.

Scott Gregory Lawrence, beloved father, son, brother,
husband and soulmate.

Soulmate. I promised him forever. Why can't anyone else see that? "I hurt Jackson. That fact devastates me. I also hurt   myself in the process. I'm a bit of a mess." A lay my head back trying to feel close.

"Cassandra thinks I'm wrong. I don't know what I think   anymore. I'm too tired from so many days of crying to think anymore. I wish you were here to talk to me. To help me." I look up. As always, nothing.

I must fall asleep because I'm startled awake when I hear voices. I open my eyes and see Harley, Reagan and Skylar standing over me. I haven't been here with them since the day of the funeral. I come on Fridays. They come when they can. We all spend time with Scott in our own ways at our own times.

I sit up, while Harley sits down next to me and puts her arm around me. "Mom, what the hell are you doing?" Reagan and Skylar sit too.

"I'm visiting your father like I do every Friday morning."

"I mean what the hell are you doing with your life?" I look at her in question. "Aunt Cass called us this morning. She told us about what happened with Jackson."

"Oh." Cass and her big mouth.

Reagan grabs my hand. "Mom, do you love Jackson? Do you want to marry him?"

"Yes, I love him, but I can't marry him. I'm married to another man. Your father."

The girls all look at each other and seem to communicate something. I don't know what. Harley nods at Skylar.

Skylar pulls a folded piece of paper from her pocket. "Mom, did you ever wonder why we show you all of our letters from Dad, except our first letter from him after he died?"

"Of course, but I assumed he wrote something about it being your obligation to take care of me and you didn't want me to see that. You didn't want me to feel like a burden."

"Well, that's not exactly right. Here's mine. Read paragraph six. Harley and Reagan had the same exact paragraph in theirs."

I scroll down to the sixth paragraph.

> *A time is going to come when your mother finds love again. She's going to doubt it because of me. She's so fiercely loyal that she's going to have a crisis of conscience. She's going to talk*

herself out of her own happiness, putting me first, as always. I can't predict the future, and I can't   describe exactly what it will look like, but it will happen.   I trust you to recognize when it does. I trust you to recognize the moment she needs to hear from me. When this happens, please give your mother the enclosed letter, titled 'For Darian, When You Find Love Again'. I trust you to give her the support she needs.

I read it three times. I look at each of the girls and Harley reaches into her pocket and pulls out an envelope. She hands it to me. My hands are shaking as I take it. Sure enough, the front reads, in Scott's handwriting, 'For Darian, When You Find Love Again'.

I just stare at the envelope. I can't believe I'm about to hear from Scott again after nearly three and a half years.

Harley stands and grabs her sisters' hands. "We're going to give you some privacy. We'll be waiting for you by the car." They walk away, leaving me with my letter. I'm trembling as I open the envelope. I pull the letter out. There are already tears rolling down my cheeks.

> *Darian:*
>
> *My love. You were the best wife a man could ever have. I'm so fortunate for the time we had*

together. You are   beautiful, sexy, smart, funny, an amazing mother, and so very loyal. You're the whole package. I knew it the moment I saw you in the library all those years ago. That's why I stalked you for weeks. You took my breath away, and I didn't think I deserved you. I was too much of a chicken to ask you out. I thank my lucky stars that I finally got the courage and did. I still can't believe you said yes.

The very first time I touched you, I knew I would never touch another woman for the rest of my life. When you've got perfection, there's no reason to even consider anything else.

If you're receiving this letter, a few things have   happened. First, I am no longer physically with you. I'm so sorry baby. I tried to eat healthily and exercise, but those Lawrence genes are a little too strong.

Second, you've found someone else that our children think you should be with. He must be pretty damn special if our kids think him deserving of you. I want you to know something. Darian, it's okay. I'm okay with it. I want you to find love again and live a full life. Life is too precious to dwell on the past. As much as it pains me to say it, I'm your past. This lucky bastard is your future. Love him. Let him love you. Be with him in any way you want, even marriage.

Hear me, Darian. If you find a man who will treat you like the queen you are, and you truly love him, it's okay with me if you marry him. You have my permission. When the day comes that my gorgeous girl is walking down the aisle again, I'll be the one giving you away. You're mine to give away, and I'm doing it. Darian, I'm giving you away to another man who can give you what I can't.

You tell him that if he ever hurts you, I will haunt him for all of eternity. But if you love him, and our kids know it's time for you to read this letter, then I know what kind of man I'm dealing with.

I'm releasing you, Darian. Live your life to the fullest.

> *I love you forever,*
> *Scott*

My face is completely covered in tears. I reread it at least twenty times. Oh, Scott. Even in death, you're putting me first.

I eventually stand up and blow him a kiss. "Bye baby. I love you always. I'll see you next Friday." I walk toward the girls. They all hug me and look down toward the letter. I hand it to them to read. They all cry while reading it. The four of us stand there holding each other sobbing.

Reagan wipes away her tears first. She straightens her back and puts out her hand for me. "Let's go get him back." Harley nods. Skylar nods. I nod.

Harley asks, "so what do we have in mind?"

I smile. "I know exactly what to do."

CHAPTER 20

Darian

I pull up to Payton's house and knock on the door. He opens it and gives me a weak smile. "Hey, Darian."

"Hey, Payton." He's clearly uncomfortable around me right now. "Here's everything you need for tomorrow." I hand him a thick envelope. "Did you get my text yesterday with all of the instructions?"

"Yes, I received it. Honestly, Darian, I don't know if I can get him out of bed. He hasn't moved since you guys got back from Colorado." I close my eyes. My poor man. I've hurt him so much. "You broke him. I've never seen him like this. He's talking about giving me the company and moving away so he doesn't have to run into you." I can physically feel my heart constricting.

I put my hand on his shoulder. "Payton, I'm going to unbreak him. I promise. Just get him there. And he would never leave you boys. He's just hurting right now."

"I know he wouldn't leave.

"You'll get him there?"

"I'll try."

Jackson

I can't believe I've agreed to this. I obviously want to spend time with my boys, but going to an Eagles football game is just about the last thing I need to be doing right now.

Payton said it was an additional Christmas present that they've all been working on for months. He went on and on about how they got amazing field-level seats, on the fifty-yard line, and that it's a once-in-a-lifetime opportunity. I don't want to be here, but I couldn't disappoint them. At least I know I won't see Darian here. She hates the Eagles.

I haven't left my house in nearly a week. I'm a shell of a man right now. I told Payton I might need to leave the area. I can't bear to see her, especially if she starts dating another man. But I know I won't leave my sons. I'm about to become a grandfather. I want to be here with all of them.

I'm sitting in my seat, not particularly paying attention to the game when I hear our entire section start booing. I look up to the game to see what I missed, but there's no action right now. It looks like a timeout on the field. What are they booing?

They all seem to be looking at someone walking down the steps. I stand up to have a look, and I see Darian and her girls walking down the steps. She's wearing a Washington jersey, so all the Philly fans are booing her. What the hell is she doing here? She walks straight toward me with a smile on her face. She's so beautiful. I miss her face. I miss all of her.

She stands in front of me. "Hey, Jackson."

I look down. I can't look at her in the eyes. I mumble, "why are you here, Darian?"

"I'm here for you." What? She tilts my chin so that I'm forced to look at her in the eyes, then she takes my hands in hers. "Jackson, I made a mistake. I want to marry you."

I don't understand. "I'm confused. What about what you said about Scott?"

She takes a deep breath. "I guess I'm just one of those lucky people who get two loves of my life. He was my soulmate and the love of the first half of my life. You, Jackson, are my soulmate and the love of the rest of my life. Hear me, Jackson. I do love you with my *whole* heart. It's yours. I'm yours if you'll still have me."

It's then that I notice that we're on the jumbotron and the entire stadium is watching us. She gets down on one knee. "Jackson Knight, will you let me love you for the rest of our lives. Will you let me be your wife? Will you marry me?"

I'm stunned into silence. A Philly fan yells out, "don't say yes to a Washington fan." We all laugh, breaking the tension.

I look at her. My everything. My soulmate. I feel the corner of my mouth tilt up. "I should say no so you have to be on blooper reels for the rest of your life."

She smiles. It's magnificent. I'm a goner. She squeezes my hands in hers. "Is that your answer? Sixty-five thousand of our closest friends are waiting for your answer, Knight."

I look down at her for one more tortuous moment and then I bend down to take her lips in mine. The whole stadium starts cheering.

I pull her up and wrap her legs around my waist. Now we're really kissing. Open-mouthed, tongue kissing. The crowd cheers even louder. 'I Don't Want To Miss A Thing' by   Aerosmith is playing on the loudspeakers.

I hear Reagan. "Oh shit, here they go again. And we're going to have to relive this on TV for the rest of our lives."

We laugh into each other's mouths. She looks at me and holds my face in her hands. "Is that a yes?"

"Darian, you're the love of my life. My soulmate. Of course, it's a yes."

EPILOGUE

Two Months Later

Darian

"Hey, baby. I want to introduce you to someone today." I take Jackson's hand. "This is Jackson, and I'm madly in love with him. We're getting married next week. We're doing a small family wedding in Mexico. We're all going to spend the week down there. Our girls couldn't be happier about it. They adore Jackson. Now they're getting the brothers they've always wanted." I smile at Jackson.

He puts his hand on the tombstone. "Nice to meet you, Scott. I want to thank you for helping us to get here. Obviously, you knew Darian well enough to know what she needed to be happy. I want you to know that I've got it from here. I'm going to make her happy for the rest of her life. I love her with every ounce of myself. She will never need for anything a day in her life. I promise to treat her like the queen she is." Tears are streaming down my cheeks at his reference to Scott's words in his letter.

I touch the tombstone too. "Bye baby. I love you always. I won't see you next Friday, but I'll be back to update you on the girls in a few weeks." Jackson and I walk away arm in arm with my head on his shoulder. I notice that there are lots of birds flying around over us.

One Week Later

Jackson

My bride is walking down the aisle. She's so beautiful in a short, casual white dress, holding a bouquet of tulips. Her girls are in similar dresses, but with color. They're already standing up here.

My boys are next to me in colorful linen shirts and khaki pants. I'm in a white linen shirt and khaki pants. Trevor was the self-appointed flower girl. He made a spectacle of himself walking down the aisle to rap music while throwing flowers everywhere.

Cassandra, Darian's parents, a clearly pregnant Kylie, my father, Donna, Darian's brother, Will and his family are our only guests. I rented us all a giant private villa, and we've had a week full of fun, food, laughter, drinks and love. The wedding ceremony is the culmination of this

amazing week. Everyone is leaving tomorrow except Darian and me. We're staying another week in paradise.

Just before Darian gets to me, she looks to her side in silent acknowledgment of the person we know is giving her away. Then she looks up at me and smiles. I grab her in my arms and kiss her. I hear Reagan snicker, "they're not even going to make it through the ceremony." Everyone laughs.

We recite our vows and promise to love each other until death does us part. When I'm told that I can kiss my bride, I pick her up in my arms and kiss the shit out of her. Cassandra and Trevor both yell at the same time "get a room." We break from our kiss in time for me to see Cassandra wink at Trevor. I don't even want to know what that's about. Everyone claps and cheers for us.

We've danced the night away, but now it's time for Darian and me to be alone. I assume she wants to make slow, sweet love tonight.

I climb up on the bed with my back to the headboard. I see her plug something into the side of the TV, and then she comes and sits between my legs. Her back to my front. I'm kissing her neck and slowly pulling up her dress with my hands on her thighs and hips.

She fiddles with the remote control and then I see what's going on. On the TV is the video of us from Club Yeur. She turns her head around and kisses me. While running her tongue along my lips, she whispers, "I want to reenact that night, Jackson." Her wish is my command. God, I love this woman.

THE END

If you'd like to continue to read about the Knight and Lawrence gangs, Dr. Harley will be the next book in the series. It will be available in the summer of 2022. Turn the page to read the prologue.

SNEAK PEEK

Book 2: Dr. Harley

Prologue

THE PAST ~ THREE YEARS AGO

Harley

"Reagan, you don't need to transfer here. Stay where you are. Skylar and I can handle things." I'm on the phone, walking down the sidewalk in high heels, trying not to bump into people.

"Harley, Mom is a disaster. Dad died a month ago, and the only time she has left the house has been for the funeral and her weekly visits to his grave. She barely leaves her bedroom. She won't even consider going into the family room of her own house." That's where she found Dad. He collapsed after having a heart attack. He was already gone by the time she found him.

"You don't need to do this. We've got it."

"Skylar is only just starting college. She's going to be busy   making new friends, rushing, going to parties, and things like that. You've got your second year of medical school about to begin. You guys won't have time."

"You're in college too, Reagan."

"I know, but I think the three of us can cover more territory. Between our three busy schedules, one of us should be   available at most times to check on Mom. Aunt Cass is sleeping there, so she's got the nights and early mornings covered." She pauses for a moment. "Harley, I just need to be here in town for her right now. She needs all of us."

I sigh. "I guess I understand. I feel bad though. You love school so much." The volume of the music increases as I get closer to the club.

"I'm fine with it. Really. I know a ton of people here. My plan is to open a business in Philly anyway. I can make some good contacts by going to school here. The transfer paperwork has already been filed. I start in a week." The music picks up. "Where the hell are you? It sounds like my freshman dorm on a Thursday night."

"I'm meeting Angelina and some of the girls at Club Liberty tonight."

"You're going out? Let me mark this date on my calendar."

"Very funny. Medical school starts back up on

Monday. I'll be buried in books in no time. The past month has been nothing short of hell. I need one night to have a few drinks and have a little fun."

"Why the fuck wasn't I invited? I'm the most fun person you know." This is true. I wish I could let loose and have fun like Reagan. I've never been like that. I've always been focused on my studies.

"Sorry. It was last minute. The girls actually pushed me to go out. They said they know this will be my last night of fun for a year." Unfortunately, this is also true.

"Good. I'm glad. Do shots, dance up a storm, and find yourself a man. You could use a little action." She pauses for a moment. "Actually, I could use some too."

I smile and shake my head. I wish I could. "Not really my style, but I'll definitely have a few drinks and dance."

"I'm telling Aunt Cass on you."

I laugh. "No no. I don't need her meddling. I'll compromise and dance with a few guys. I promise."

"Do more than dance with them."

I shake my head. "Good-bye. I'll see you at Mom's tomorrow."

"See you then."

I spot Angelina, Olivia and Sophie waiting for me out front. "Sorry I'm late."

Angelina looks at her watch. "You're literally exactly on time." That's late for me. "You look hot. Nicely done. Let's go have some fun." I'm wearing a short tight royal blue dress that more than shows off my figure. It's low cut and my boobs are practically spilling out. Reagan bought it for me for Christmas last year. It's not something I would normally wear. This is the first time I've ever worn it.

The bouncer lets us butt in front of the line. It's the one perk of being fairly attractive. No lines. We head straight to the bar and order eight lemon drop shots and four margaritas. The bartender brings us our drinks. Olivia holds a shot glass up in the air. "To Harley actually being out." We all clink glasses and down the shot.

Sophie holds the second shot glass up in the air. "To Harley letting loose." The three of them hold their shot glasses up. I stare at them. "Come on Harley. Just one night. Forget the past month. Forget studying. Live in the moment. Do something just because it feels good." I reluctantly hold my shot glass up with theirs. They all smile. "That's my girl!" We down the   second round of shots, followed quickly thereafter by our margaritas.

Angelina grabs my hand. "Let's dance."We dance for over two hours, taking breaks here and there for drinks. We're having a great time. There are a lot of men surrounding our group trying jump in, but we pay them no attention. We're doing our own thing tonight.

I offer to go buy the next round. I head to the bar and order four more margaritas. The bartender brings me the drinks and I go to hand her my credit card. A big hand grabs mine from behind and I hear him say, "I've got it." He attempts to hand the   bartender his card instead.

I shake my head. "No thanks, *I've* got it." I give her my card and she leaves to ring it up.

The man chuckles. I turn around and look up and up until I'm met with big blue eyes. I see him smiling. "Wow, you and your friends are really putting out the 'fuck off' vibe tonight."

I laugh. "Yea, we're just here letting off some steam. Not   looking for extra company." He smiles again. He's really   attractive. He's very tall, with wavy blonde hair, and a square chin with a dimple.

"I don't think those guys got the memo." He points his thumb to my friends. There's a circle of at least ten guys around them. "You and your friends haven't let them in for one dance, and yet they just stand there waiting like puppy dogs."

I laugh. "That's life in the big city."

"More like the life of beautiful women in the big city. One in particular."

We're uncomfortably silent for a moment. "Like I said, we're just here to have a bit of fun together. We've all got some things going on and we're looking to have a rare good time with close friends."

His face gets serious for a moment. "What do you have going on that you can't have a good time? You should always make time for a little fun."

"Nothing I'm interested in discussing. Nice to meet you. I'm going to head back to my friends." I go to grab the drinks, but he stops me.

"We didn't really meet. I don't know your name. You don't know mine." We stare at one another for a few moments. He's really cute. If I actually had time in my life to date, I'd be into this guy, but I don't. "I'm Brody by the way."

I grab the drinks and wave with an open finger. "Bye Brody." I walk away and head back to my friends to give them their margaritas.

We're back dancing in our own world when I feel big hands on my shoulders and hot breath on my ear. "You forgot   something." I turn around and Brody is holding up my credit card. Whoops. I must have left it at the bar. I go to grab it, but he pulls it away. "One dance. I'll give it back to you if you dance with me for one song."

I roll my eyes. "Fine. One song." One dance with a hot guy won't kill me. I promised that to Reagan anyway.

A slow sensual song starts playing. Figures. I go to put my hands on his shoulders but he grabs my shoulders and turns me around. He wraps his arms around me and pulls my back to his chest. My hips to his. My backside to his front. He starts moving us in rhythm together, swaying to the slow beat of the music. We stay like that for a while. He starts moving his hands up and down my hips, and runs his lips along my neck. I close my eyes. God this feels good. He feels good. Before I know it, three songs have gone by and we haven't moved from this position. He whispers in my ear. "Come home with me."

That breaks my momentary trance. I turn around and put my hands on my hips. "You've got the wrong girl, buddy." I hold out my hand for the card. He gives it to me.

I turn to leave but he puts his hand on the small of my back and pulls me close to him, locking his eyes with mine. He's silent for a moment, doing nothing but staring at me. He takes his other hand and gently runs his thumb across my bottom lip. "You are so incredibly beautiful." He bends down and takes my bottom lip into his mouth and slowly sucks it. I close my eyes and moan at the sensation. I can feel it in my whole body. I have a strong ache forming between my legs.

I have no idea what comes over me. Maybe it's the alcohol. Maybe it's the emotions of the past month. Maybe it's the fact that I know I'll be buried in my studies in a few days. Maybe it's the insanely hot guy sucking on my lip. Maybe it's my pledge to do something that just feels good tonight. Whatever it is, I grab his hand and lead him into the stairwell. We walk up two flights of stairs in silence to the roof. There are several large, wide columns up on the roof affording some privacy from the outside world.

I push him against the wall of one of the columns, grab his face and crash my lips to his. Our mouths immediately open. Our tongues relentlessly exploring one another. The kiss is passionate and warm, yet his lips are soft and tender. He grabs my waist and pulls me close. I run my hands up through his hair, grabbing it by the handful. He turns us so that my back is now to the wall, and pushes himself against me. I can feel his massive erection on my stomach.

He slowly moves his hands up my body and grabs my breasts. Even though he has big hands, they're still not big enough to fit around my breasts. He yanks my dress and bra down so that my breasts pop out. He pulls away from my lips and looks down, slowly running his fingertips around my chest, and brushing his thumbs across my nipples. They harden immediately. "You have the most perfect body I've ever seen."

He bends his head down and takes one of my nipples into his warm mouth. He sucks it hard. I lay my head back on the wall and moan in pleasure. He moves along to the other nipple, and gives it the same heavenly treatment. It feels so good. He gets down on his knees as he kisses his way down my body. He slowly pulls the bottom of my dress up to my waist. He runs his fingers up my legs until he reaches my white lace thong. He pulls it down my legs and off my body. He rolls it up and puts it in his pocket.

He open mouth kisses his way up from my knees to the apex of my thighs. He throws one of my legs over his shoulder and moves the other leg out wide. He spreads my lips and takes a long lick.

"Oh God," I moan. He smiles up at me for a brief moment, and then brings his mouth back to me again. He's moving his tongue up and down, licking me everywhere. He starts sucking on my clit. I'm on stimulation overload. I don't even know the last time I came, but it's definitely going to happen for me now.

He takes one of his thumbs and slides it through me until it's at my entrance. He slowly pushes it in. The dual sensation feels too good. I don't think I can stand on my one leg anymore. He must sense it because he throws that leg over his shoulder too. He's supporting me on his shoulders, and using the wall to support my back. I don't know how he's doing it. I don't care.

He continues alternating licking and sucking my clit, while pumping me with his thumb, until I can feel myself starting to slip over the edge. I feel my walls trembling. A few more licks and pumps, and I explode on his tongue and thumb with a very loud moan. I think I nearly blackout from the pleasure. He lets me ride out my orgasm as he continues to lick up my juices.

He gradually sets my shaky legs down. I'm not sure I can fully stand, but I use the wall to lean back and support most of my weight. I'm panting, and I didn't even do anything. I can't see straight yet. I hear his belt buckle and zipper, and then the tearing open of a condom wrapper. He kisses my mouth again and whispers into it. "Are you with me? I'm not done with you." I nod at a loss for words. I'm not done yet either. I need him inside of me.

I feel him grab the underside of my ass with

two hands, spread my legs, and pick me up. My senses are starting to come back to me. I wrap my legs around him. His tip is at my entrance as he slowly enters me. He keeps going and going and going. Oh shit. He must be huge. I didn't even see him before he entered me, but I've never felt anything so big inside of me. It's all-encompassing.

Once he's all the way in, he stops. I'm looking down hoping this sucker is actually all the way in. I don't think I can take any more, but it's stretching me in the best way possible. I feel the pleasure slowly spreading throughout my body. He removes one hand from my ass and he tilts my chin up so that I'm   looking at him. "Are you okay?"

I wrap my arms around his neck, kissing my way up to his ear. I whisper, "God yes. I'm good. Please keep going." He starts pumping into me. In and out. I'm so full of him. It feels   amazing.

I grab his cheeks and bite his bottom lip. I move down to his neck. He tastes good. He smells good too. I'm sucking on his neck. He moans out in pleasure. "You feel incredible. You're so tight and wet. You're squeezing me so hard."

I throw my head back. This is too much. I'm going to come again. I've never come this quickly from penetrative sex.

With my head back, he moves onto my neck and kisses his way down to my breasts again. He circles my nipple with his tongue. He takes my nipple into his mouth. Once he sucks on it, that's my tipping point. "Ah, Brody. I'm coming." I hold onto his shirt for dear life and squeeze my eyes shut. I feel myself pulse and then explode. The sensation is indescribable. He continues to moan loudly, until he grunts into his own release.

We are still for a few moments, as we both pant and regain an awareness of our surroundings. As my senses return, I realize that I just had sex with a complete stranger. I can't believe I did that. I've never done anything like this before in my life. He slowly pulls out, and sets my legs on the ground. I fix my dress as he pulls off the condom and zips up his pants.

He gives me a soft kiss on my lips. As he moves away, he tilts his head to the side and pulls his eyebrows together. "What's your name?" Oh. My. God. I never even gave him my name, and just had mind-blowing sex with him on the roof of a club. Who am I right now?

I take a breath and then a big gulp. "Let's not go there. We both know exactly what this was. Let's not spoil it."

He looks a little sad and shrugs his shoulders. "If

that's what you want."

"It is." I fidget for a moment and then look up at him with my hand out. "Can I have my underwear back?"

He smiles. "No, beautiful. I need to hold onto something from tonight." It's not worth arguing with him. I just want to get away from him as quickly as possible.

He leads me back into the stairwell. We reach the dance floor. I see my friends and turn to him. "Bye Brody. Have a good life." I head back to my friends to finish out the evening and head home.

It's Sunday night and I'm heading to Mom's for dinner. Aunt Cass said she was just ordering Chinese food since there's no way Mom is up for cooking, and Aunt Cass doesn't know what to do in a kitchen. I have no clue what I'm walking into.   Hopefully, Mom is in a better mood and is out of bed.I open the door and walk into the house. Aunt Cass, Skylar and Reagan are all sitting at the kitchen table. No Mom. Damn. When will she snap out of this?

Reagan looks me up and down and squints her eyes. "You had sex."

My eyes pop wide open. "What? No, I didn't."

Aunt Cass turns her head to me and also looks me up and down. "Yes, you totally did." Skylar nods in agreement.

I stare at them all. "Are you three witches?"

Reagan turns to Aunt Cass "That sounds like a yes to me."

Aunt Cass nods. "Sure does. Good for you, kiddo."

I sit down and sigh. "How the hell do you guys know? Am I wearing a sign?"

Aunt Cass grabs my hand. "Harley, I love you like you're my own, but you are the most uptight woman on the face of the planet. There is something bizarrely relaxed about you right now. Something that only a good time in the sheets could   possibly achieve. Frankly, it's unsettling to see you like this." She smirks at me.

I roll my eyes. "I'm not that uptight."

Skylar and Reagan respond in unison. "Yes, you are."

Reagan couldn't possibly be more excited. "So, did you bring in a bench player or someone new?" She thinks she's making a joke.

"I met a guy at the club last night."

Reagan looks shocked. "What was his name?"

"Brody."

"Brody what?"

I look down, preferring not to answer that. She's staring at me, clearly not letting me get away with avoiding the question. I mumble, "I didn't get his last name."

She has a huge grin on her face. "I'm sorry, who are you and what have you done with my sister?"

Skylar jumps in. "Seriously Harley. That's so unlike you." She smiles at Reagan and Aunt Cass. "I'm so excited."

"You guys make me sound like a prude."

Reagan rolls her eyes. "We didn't say that you're a prude. You've just never had sex with someone you weren't in a   relationship with. You're a serial monogamist."

Aunt Cass shivers. "Ugh, monogamy. Don't use that word in my presence."

"Fine, I agree. It wasn't like me. But I did it, so deal with it."

"How was it?" Reagan just wants details.

I blow out a long breath. "Really fucking good. Like best sex of my life good."

She smiles. "Are you going to see him again?"

your mother is a shell of herself right now. only forty-five and she lost the love of her ust give her some time. She'll be back to her wesome self in no time. I promise." I hope right.

Monday morning. My first day of the second of medical school. I see my friend Megan en I walk in. "Hey Meg. What class do you e this morning?"

ey babe. I have neuro."

e too. Who do you have?"

have Dr. Waters." She scrunches up her nose. had him last year too, for anatomy. He's old as rt and boring as fuck." He's actually only in his rties, but he's definitely a boring teacher. He's little creepy too. He used to stare at me and nnecessarily touch my arm whenever he was ear me.

'True, he is a bit dull. I must be in a different section this year. I have the new professor, Dr. Cooper. He's supposed to be the best spinal surgeon in the country. I heard he's young, so maybe he'll be more interesting."

"Hope so. I'll see you for lunch?"

"Yep, see you then."

"No."

"He didn't want your number? I f
believe. Look at you."

"I didn't give him the chance. I
give him my name." I pause for a
making eye contact with any of t
was against the wall on the roof of t

Reagan, Skylar and Aunt Cass look at
with their mouths wide open in sh
turns back. "I'm not even joking. Wl
Where's Harley?"

"Shut up." I put my head in my hand
know what came over me."

"Sounds like he came over you, or was
you?" Skylar is clearly amusing herself.

I give her a nasty look. "The last month h
hell. I lost my father. I have a shell of a r
I'm about to start a   hellis
of studying with no chance at dating. A gor
guy wanted me, and I went with it. For th
time in my life, I went with it. It was great. I
more than great. But it's over now. School st
tomorrow. Back to the grind."

Reagan rubs my back. "Good. For. You, sis.
thrilled for you."

Aunt Cass grabs all of our hands, looking sad.

I make my way into the classroom. The professor hasn't   arrived yet. I sit front and center, as always. Students are filing in. Though there are plenty of empty seats, two guys sit on either side of me and smile at me. I roll my eyes. The classroom eventually fills and it's 8:00, our start time. There's a faculty only door at the front of the classroom. It opens, and a tall man walks through with his head down. He eventually looks up at no one in particular and smiles. "Good morning class. I'm Dr. Cooper."

Oh my fucking God. It's Brody. He sets his stuff down and then looks up, right at me. His smile instantly fades and his eyes just about pop out of his head in realization. I can't believe this. I had sex with my neuro professor. This is bad. Really bad.

Printed in Great Britain
by Amazon

82592983R00190